# SOCIAL MEDIA CENTRAL

## Tayler, Book One

*Kevin Klehr*

A NineStar Press Publication

Published by NineStar Press
P.O. Box 91792,
Albuquerque, New Mexico, 87199 USA.
www.ninestarpress.com

# Social Media Central



Printed in the USA
First Edition
April, 2018

Print ISBN: 978-1-948608-41-1

Also available in eBook, ISBN: 978-1-948608-37-4

In an age where everyone lives their lives through a screen, no one has more celebrity status than fashion blogger, Madeline Q. In a chance meeting, Tayler, loner and geek, is introduced to her world of parties, fan worship, and seduction.

But as his own star rises, Madeline Q is arrested for murder. There's just one problem—there is no corpse. Tayler soon learns that fiction blurs reality on Social Media Central.

# Dedication

One night in 2015, I sat sharing wine and conversation with my partner in crime, Warren, and my good friend, Clinton.

We spoke of the 'disconnect' we were seeing in society all due to the spread, and sometimes the addiction to, social media.

Then we concocted a tale about a man who lives in the future and feels the pain of this disconnect.

Little did we realize that this future was coming fast.

So this book is dedicated to my think tank, Warren and Clinton, and to this book's first editor, Jerry L. Wheeler, who made me laugh when he described this novel was "Orwellian but not."

# One

"IF THIS IS our future, then we're already dead."

I usually sat alone to eat lunch, but this man insisted on talking to me. How dare he? This was *my* park bench, *my* place of solitude, even if others were around. I politely smiled and bit into my salad sandwich, yet he continued.

"In my day, we talked to people. We knew what our neighbors were up to. The fact that we even *knew* our neighbors is a concept lost on these jokers."

I scanned the gardens. It was the same sight every day. People my age addicted to their mobile screens as if their whole world centered behind the glass face. Keystrokes and terse commands took the place of spoken feelings and thoughts.

"Smoke and mirrors for an electronic age," I replied. I took another bite.

"What's your name?" the man asked.

"Tayler. It was the name of a vlogger my mum liked."

He reached out his hand. I placed my sandwich on the brown paper bag in my lap so I could shake.

"I'm Stuart, a relic of a bygone era."

He wasn't exactly a relic. To me, old men on the scrap heap spat bitterness and ignorance in equal measure. He did neither. He was middle-aged and had the gentle face of a charity worker. But he was far from needing charity himself. His white goatee was neatly trimmed, while his thinning hair could have been just groomed by an overpriced hairdresser. And his stylish knee-length burgundy coat could've had him walking into an advertising agency as either model or executive.

He peered at the soulless beings scattered through the park, all of them representing just one of a larger tribe. Their fellow natives supplied moments of importance on the devices, and at times, their own faces signaled their moment to shine. But a new comment meant the baton had passed to the next person who needed the spotlight.

"That's why they like their small screens," said Stuart. "It presents a world bigger than them, without needing the confidence to venture into that world. Look at them. The screens are smaller than the individual. Everything in perfect proportion." He paused. "Where's your small screen?"

"I use an old phone." I pulled it from my shirt pocket. "I refuse to get involved with Social Media Central."

"Wise man." He pulled out his media device, also vintage.

"A time when a phone was just a phone," I said.

"I told you I'm a relic from the past."

"Please don't change. My landlady is about your age, and she's addicted to her cyberfriends."

"What? Doesn't she have real friends at her age?"

"She used to. I'd come home from work to the smells of her beef Wellington, her green curry, or some other culinary delight, knowing that within the half hour she'd be knocking on my door inviting me to meet some bosom buddy over dinner. And I'd return the favor. I dug out my grandma's handwritten cookbook and tried something new. My landlady would bring down one of her cats, and I shared the evening with her while she gave me advice about money or love or something."

"Love? With your looks, you don't seem like a lad who needs advice on love."

My cheeks felt warmer.

"Did your landlady break hearts?"

"She said she did, but I kept getting the impression that none of her lovers stayed around for long. We don't do dinner anymore. We haven't for two years."

"Why not?"

"Bloody Social Media Central. She lives on it. It's her whole life. She's part of a group that calls itself the Amazing Twenty. Twenty lost individuals who've never met but stay online for hours just to feel someone cares."

"What about you, Tayler? Who are your friends?"

"I don't know anymore. It's harder and harder to connect. Social Media Central has taken away the few connections I had here and made them believe they're part of that wider world you were talking about. So I sit watching old movies to pass the time. Movies that demand an attention span."

"I hear you, friend. I hear you."

People started chattering at the sight of a woman walking into the park. Her long red hair streamed like a waterfall down her neck, half covering the shapely mounds that heralded her arrival. The people of the park snapped her image as if their devices could capture true beauty.

"Madeline" they called, echoing her name around the park.

"Who is she?" I asked.

"No idea."

"A selfie, Ms. Q?" yelled one of her eager fans.

"Sweetie, I don't share selfies."

Groupies ran up to get a closer shot. One woman in a white shirt fainted in her boyfriend's arms. He dragged her to a nearby bench and laid her down. A guy with rounded glasses, similar to mine, tried to plant a kiss on her cheek.

She reached into her tiny handbag and pulled out a fan, swiping the air between him and herself. He pulled back and looked to the ground like a small boy coming to terms with adult behavior.

She then noticed me, so some of her devotees took my photo. Stuart gave me a wink as she strolled toward me.

"You don't know me, do you?"

I shook my head.

"What a weird yet reassuring surprise."

"Reassuring?"

"As you can see, my fan base likes to go nuts."

"It's your outfits, Miss," one cried. "I need to know what to wear before the season ends."

Now that two of her best assets were in my face, I breathed in the scent of her black leather top. Small laces crisscrossed her cleavage. My wayward thoughts were interrupted when she placed her long-nailed finger under my jaw. She pushed upward, raising my head to study my face.

"I'm not that easy, sweetie, even with those that intrigue me. And trust me, you intrigue me. What's your name?"

I mumbled, not making sense.

"His name's Tayler," Stuart said.

"Tayler, eh? I'm Madeline Q, queen of the universe."

"And what a small universe that must be."

"You tired old man, do you even know who I am?"

"The latest vlog sensation? The latest reality web-series loser? It doesn't matter, princess. You'll be forgotten by the end of the year."

She still pushed my jaw upward. "You think I'm special, don't you, Tayler? You may not know what power I have over these hordes, but let me assure you, I have power."

"I can, um, I can see that."

"We need to talk about this beard of yours. It's shabby chic."

"Huh?"

"It's short but not elegantly trimmed like the has-been's next to you."

"Right."

"Let me guess, you're about twenty-three?"

"Twenty-five."

"I see, only ten years younger than me. Well, Tayler, the next time we meet, and we will meet again, I want you to wear a black T-shirt. This lazy checkered top is not doing your stylishly rough metro-beard any justice."

She removed her finger and blew me a kiss. The park folk applauded, taking more snaps of us both. She presented me with a business card from her handbag, her name spelled out on the scarlet background in a classy black font I had never seen before. She turned on her heel and walked away. Others followed like kids drawn to a piper's flute.

"Well, it looks like you've been touched by celebrity of some sort or another," said Stuart. "But kids today celebrate the mundane so I'm sure her appeal has a shelf life."

I nodded, more to shut him up than to agree. I read the small print above the phone number on Madeline's card: Fashion Icon and Blogger. I then placed it carefully in my top pocket.

"What are you grinning about?"

"Stuart, I'm off to buy a black T-shirt."

# Two

MY LANDLADY, MARY, wore a revealing white dress as she sat in front of her outdated computer. With her best years behind her, the frock could not save her fallen breasts from pressing against her desk for more support.

One of her cats clawed at her bare feet, meowing as if it hadn't been fed for days. Before Mary noticed I was in the room, I went to her kitchen to find food. All I found was milk. A gluggy white custard splattered from the carton with a smell that could strip paint off a wall. I ran the tap and washed the evil mess down the sink.

"Who's there?" Mary yelled.

"Only me." I came out of the kitchen. "Have you fed your cats lately?"

"I think so. Do they look hungry?"

"One of them was scratching at your feet a moment ago. Didn't you feel it?"

She looked around. I pointed to the ginger furball that had wrapped itself around my legs.

"Oh. I'll feed them in a second. I'm just looking through Tammy's wedding photos."

"Have I met Tammy?"

I peered at the screen. A man sporting shoulder pads danced with a woman wrapped in a dress so tight, it was begging for mercy. Both looked like casting rejects from a 1980s prime-time drama about rich oil barons. As Mary flipped through the images, I noted the guests were more engaged with their screens than the couple who brought them to this moment. But at least a few paid the bride some attention by snapping her picture.

"I'm sure I haven't met her," I said. "How do you know her?"

"We chat online all the time."

"Yes, Mary, but how did you meet?"

"Right here, on Social Media Central."

The reddish feline pawed at my jeans. "Don't you think it's time to feed your cats?"

"In a moment." She closed Tammy's social page and looked at the newsfeed of a handsome man thirty years younger. In the reflection from the screen, I could see her smile like a child who'd discovered ice cream, followed with concern as if the treat had melted. "Tayler, how did you get into my apartment?"

"The door opened when I knocked. You know, you really shouldn't leave it unlocked."

"I didn't mean to. Why are you here?"

"It's rent day."

"Is it Wednesday already?"

"Yes."

"Oh."

"I'll leave the money on your dining table."

"Okay."

I left and climbed the stairs, returning shortly with some leftover chicken I was saving for dinner. As I walked in, Mary danced in stilted moves as if she was communicating in Egyptian hieroglyphics to the delighted gent on her computer. She swung her head toward the door, and our eyes met. Hers widened.

"Oh, Tayler, have you met Bernard?"

I waved at the screen. "Hi, Bernard."

"Hi, Tayler" came the voice from the tinny speaker.

"Tayler's my tenant. He's lived above me for years."

"And how do you know Bernard?"

"Social Media Central," they both replied.

I accidentally bit my tongue.

"Bernard is a...um, what is it you said you were, Bernard?"

"A dentist." He flashed his pearly whites.

"I see," I said. "Are you going somewhere tonight, Mary?"

"No." She looked puzzled.

"It's just that you've dressed up." With her face turned from the screen, she scowled at me. I handed her the plate of chicken. "This is for your cats."

"My cats? Why would I need chicken, Tayler? I have plenty of food for my dear little ones."

"Tayler's right," said Bernard. "You look radiant this evening, Mary."

"Really? Oh, it's just something I threw on. I wanted to look nice for my friends. At my age, I don't get a chance to throw on a frock anymore."

"Then maybe we should do dinner together?"

"Yes, we could mirror meal."

"Mirror meal?" I asked.

"Really, Tayler, you're so out of touch."

"How about steak, mash, and gravy?" Bernard asked.

"Yes, I can make that. I'd light candles but I don't think my camera works that well with mood lighting."

"That's fine. I'll bring the music. I'll make up a special playlist and stream it through as we eat."

"Then it's a date. How does seven p.m. tomorrow sound?"

"I can't tomorrow, my love. I have another appointment."

"Not another woman?"

"No, nothing like that. I'm overdue with my taxes, so I'm linking up with my accountant in the evening."

"We can have a late supper."

"No, let's mirror meal on Friday. That way we both won't be dateless over the weekend."

"Sounds perfect." She placed the plate of chicken next to the computer. "Tayler, why is your mouth open like that?"

"Sorry, I'm in shock. Let me get this straight. Instead of going out for dinner, you're both cooking steak and mashed potato and eating in front of your computer screens. Oh, brother. Let me take an educated guess. You two have never met face to face."

"Tayler, don't be so rude," my landlady said.

"That's okay, Mary. My son, Mike, is just like Tayler. Out of touch with technological trends. No offense, Tayler."

"None taken."

"Mary, my darling, I have to go. Tammy is trying to get my attention."

"I was just looking at her wedding photos. Put her through. We can both talk to her."

"I can't really do that. She's marked her contact request as *private*. Between you and me, I think she married prematurely. There were already problems in their relationship, but she went ahead with the ceremony anyway."

"I understand, my darling." Mary lost her smile momentarily. "I'm looking forward to Friday."

"So am I, my love."

"Bye, Bernard, until—" Her cyberboyfriend disappeared. "Oh, damn these bad connections. The government needs to get this right."

I placed my hand on her shoulder. She didn't respond. "So was it love at first sight?"

"Not quite." She seemed oblivious to my sarcasm. "But I knew there was a special connection the first time we video chatted."

"Has he met the Amazing Twenty?"

My hand slipped from her as she stepped forward. "Tayler, *he* came up with the name. Without him, I wouldn't have met the others."

"Has he got legs?"

"Tayler!"

"I'm just asking. I mean, have you ever video chatted with him doing anything other than sitting down?"

"I think so. Hmm." She rested her finger on her chin. "Oh, Tayler, why can't you just be happy I'm in love?"

"So, Bernard is the reason the Amazing Twenty exists. How did you find him?"

"We told you. Through Social Media Central."

"Yes, but through which application?"

She beamed.

"Oh I see. Through *Lover Net*. Does he blog about his pursuits?"

"He used to."

"Does he blog about you?"

"Sort of. He calls me *the sophisticated lady* in his posts."

I tried to keep a straight face.

"Oh, Tayler, don't rain on my parade just because I have someone and you don't. Love will tap you on the shoulder one day. Isn't that what I always say to you?"

I missed the landlady I used to dine with—the woman whose wisdom had turned to mainstream quotes since she discovered Social Media Central. I wanted to say, "Step into the real world," but there was less and less real world to step into.

I eyed the untouched chicken next to the beast that had taken her soul. Some of her cats were gazing at it too, while Mary swayed, blissfully unaware of their hunger.

I grabbed the plate, headed for the kitchen, and pulled out various unmatched bowls. The pets purred desperately as if I was their savior. When I bent down to place their dinner on the floor, the card that fashion blogger had given me slipped from my shirt pocket. Once again I noticed the bold lettering stood out against the richly colored background. I picked it up and held it while the cats devoured their meals like addicts.

"Mary," I called, "do you know Madeline Q?"

"Everyone knows Madeline Q."

"I don't." I joined her in the living room where she was already hard at work moving her mouse.

"Anyone who knows anything about anyone, Tayler, knows who Madeline Q is. She's a fashion blogger. Why do you ask?"

"I met her today."

Her eyes widened. "My dear, you've met royalty."

"From what country?"

"No, no, Tayler. She's a social media celebrity. Don't you know anything? She hangs around with the cream of the cybercrop."

"The cybercrop? Is that what you young kids are calling it these days?"

"My god! The person who gives me rent met Madeline Q, yet he has no idea who she is. What's that in your hand? Is that her card?" I showed it to her, but she started reciting the phone number so I pulled it away. "You have to ring her. Bring her to your apartment. I'll pay for the redecorating."

"I've lived there for years, and you've never offered to fix the place up."

"That's because you were a no one. Now you're a someone."

I chuckled even though her comment made me sad. I glanced at the card. "Wow, Mary. Glad you think I'm worth knowing. Like old times, isn't it?"

Her mouth opened, but no words came out. I left and skipped up the stairs. The moment my door was closed, I leaned against it, pulled out my phone, and dialed Madeline Q's number.

# Three

"I'M LOOKING FOR Madeline Q."

"Everyone's looking for Madeline Q," the bald woman at the door said to me.

I pulled out the fashion blogger's business card.

"Oh, you *are* looking for Madeline Q. Not sure about your outfit, though. Didn't she tell you tonight's theme is Eros?"

"I'm bare-chested."

"Suspenders and jeans do not make an outfit." Behind her were several rustic shelves stacked with black clothing. She handed me a pair of leather pants, which unfolded when I grabbed them.

"There's no crotch in these."

"Exactly! What did you expect?"

"My underwear's white. This will look stupid."

"Foolish boy, you don't wear underpants with those."

"What kind of party is this?"

"You want to be the talk of the cyberworld, don't you?"

I handed the fetish-wear back.

"Or don't we measure up?" she said.

"What about that hat on the top shelf?"

"You mean the cap? Hmm. Does your master know you're out alone tonight?"

"What?"

She threw it like a Frisbee in my direction. I caught it and popped it on. She then waved her arm toward the red door as if all the treasures of the world were waiting inside. As I opened it, a flash of light blinded me.

"That's hardly a pout," said a male voice.

When I could see again, I noticed a well-groomed man of Middle Eastern appearance about to snap me once more with his massive camera.

"Hold on," I said. "Wait until my sight returns."

I stepped forward. He was clearer now. His thick, dark hair glistened as much as his trimmed, dense beard. In fact, his mane looked a little bluish as dim light highlighted its sheen.

Frayed jeans brushed the tops of his bare feet, designer rips all over the denim. A formal waistcoat covered his chest with two stylish buttons. And somehow he still managed to see properly through his square-ish sunglasses as he attained the charisma of an industry-manufactured pop star.

"That's better," he said. "But it's still not perfect. Give me your orgasm face."

"My orgasm face?"

"It's Eros night, remember?"

I played along, swaying my head back while trying not to smirk.

"You look like an opera singer. And a bad one at that." He snapped my photo again. "That's better. You're natural."

"No, I'm confused."

He reached for my hand. "Connor, official socialite photographer. I've never seen you at one of our parties before."

"I'm Tayler." I shook his hand while reaching for the business card in my jeans pocket. I held it in front of his dark shades. "This woman invited me."

"Hmm. You're a little younger than she likes them." He snapped again. "Stop waving your hands in front of your face. Yeah, that's the look I want for my blog. Think sexual thoughts."

"Is this another one of Madeline's conquests?" another voice queried.

"Are you?" Connor asked me.

"No, we've never, um, she only met me the other day."

The flash went off again. "You've lost your pout, Tayler. I think you need a cocktail." He clutched my wrist.

"Don't worry, we'll look after you until Ms. Q remembers who you are," that other voice said. It belonged to a thirty-something man sporting a buzz cut that extended to his goatee, all slightly reddish. He seemed the type of guy who could hold his own in a street fight, but his cheeky grin got to me. It was the type of smile an older brother gives when reassuring a sibling.

I then noted the perfectly outlined Superman symbol on his bare chest, along with his studded belt, blue jeans, and black leather shoes. "Very clever."

"This is Shaun," said Connor. "The jet-setting explorer."

"I'd shake your hand, Tayler, but—" He raised two garishly green drinks. "Looks like I'm Connor's private butler again."

"Shaun, if you were my butler, I'd make you pick the pubes from my shower drain, not carry around my drink."

"Thank god for small mercies."

"How did you get that superhero logo so perfect?" I asked.

"My girlfriend painted it on with her makeup."

"This week's girlfriend, he means," Connor added.

"Where is she?" I asked.

"She's here somewhere, probably finding her next conquest."

"Haven't you read about her, Tayler?"

Connor and Shaun exchanged puzzled glances as I casually took in the festivities. An array of spotlights threw beams in all directions, giving glimpses of a room decorated solely in black and gold. Vintage tassels, strips of leather and elaborate headwear competed for attention with the dozen or so guests who opted for naked flesh. White powders and pills spread across a coffee table enticed many, like beasts to a watering hole on a steamy day.

The space throbbed with a heavy beat. Mating dances of all persuasions took place right next to people conversing. One woman swayed her hips as if she was peeling off seven imaginary veils, while a horny array of gents and ladies emulated her hypnotic moves.

"Whose party is this, anyway?" Connor asked.

"Someone trying to be us," Shaun replied.

"Could it be that lost boy over there on the couch wearing golden deer horns and holding the flute?"

"Now, Connor, play nice. Just because he's not your type."

"I *was* being nice. He seems like the type who wants to break into SMC."

"SMC?" I asked. "Oh, Social Media Central."

"So you do know us," said Shaun. I shook my head. "I think we have a virgin here."

"Personally, it's refreshing to meet someone who doesn't know who we are," said Connor. He took our picture.

"It's not like Madeline to invite someone fresh." Shaun gave me a wink. "What's she up to?"

"You know, I think I can make that deer-horned boy a sparkling star, briefly."

"Watch out, Tayler. Connor has a new project."

"I'll be back in a moment." Connor strayed off.

"What about your drink?" Shaun called to the wandering photographer.

"Give it to Tayler."

Connor weaved through the crowd like the messiah. Would-be glamour models froze in outlandish poses. They lost their cheesy grins the moment he moved on to his next starlets. Deer-horned boy eyed him warily, so the photographer offered his hand.

"So, you're a traveler, Shaun?"

"No. Where did you get that idea?"

"Connor introduced you as a jet-setting explorer."

"Oh, don't mind him. It's just his brand of humor." He looked into the crowd. "I explore a lot. But I don't jet-set." He stopped watching Connors exploits. "You're not getting this, are you?"

"Well, you are talking in riddles."

"How much do you know about Social Media Central? I mean, I take it you're not the online kind."

"No, I'm not."

"Have you heard of Lover Net?"

I groaned. "My landlady thinks she's found the man of her dreams, but they've never met beyond webcam."

"Well, Tayler, I'm not like your landlady. I meet my devotees and write about my adventures on Lover Net. And women write about me. In fact, they like to rate me, but I don't read my reviews."

"Do you rate them?"

"Never. I write about them, and only name them if they've specifically asked after reading what I've written."

"You're a cybergigolo."

"I get some money out of it, but I also get first- or business-class tickets to other parts of the world from interested followers in exchange for intimacy. I'm ethical that way. I do it to spread love."

I giggled. "Oh, you're serious."

"Okay, it sounds like I'm living the male dream, but I choose who I sleep with. If I'm contacted by someone who's interested in me, I webcam them first. Maybe even mirror-meal them." I rolled my eyes, but he didn't notice. "That way

I find the most interesting women to get to know. And let's face it, Tayler, you never really know anyone until you make love to them."

He met my gaze as if he was waiting for my reaction. If I was the type to swing both ways, I'd have been captivated. His charm was neither metrosexual nor roguish. He stood apart and yet equally at home in either camp, a man observing the world while quietly conducting it.

"Well hello!" Madeline had found us and was flaunting the back of her hand in front of my face. I kissed it. She shivered theatrically. Shaun grinned wearily.

"I'm so glad I found you," I said.

"Please, Tyler—"

"It's Tayler, Madeline."

"Please, Tayler, call me Ms. Q. I like the sound of that."

"Shouldn't you put out the fire in front of the Boy Scout?" Shaun suggested.

"He knows what he's playing with."

Two girls who were too young to be out this time of night snaked up to the fashion blogger. Both wore lacy nighties, a mistake for the one whose figure resembled a sagging balloon. As they raised their screens, Madeline raised her hand.

"You girls know my main rule!"

"Please, Madeline Q, just one selfie with us. We're your biggest fans."

"Not in those outfits, you're not."

The thinner girl slapped her comrade on the shoulder. "I told you not to wear that."

"Come now. That's not the way you treat a friend," said Shaun.

"How about a selfie with you, then?"

"Not tonight, girls."

They quickly snapped the queen of style and the womanizer. Then they took my picture. As they strolled away, the rounder one asked her companion who I was. "Search me. But he's with Madeline Q and Shaun. He has to be someone."

"So why don't you share selfies?" I asked my supposed date.

"I have standards." She and her fellow celebrity shared a knowing glance. "Tayler, I'm glad you're here. And I like what you're wearing, especially the leather cap."

"And you make that leather miniskirt sing, Ms. Q."

"This must all seem like a circus to you," said Shaun.

"A little. I just can't believe you two are so famous. I mean, it's just social media."

"Dear, it's Social Media Central," Madeline said.

"But still, it's a mind-fuck."

"Why?"

"Well, look at these people. They're a generation with shallow friendships."

"Tayler, they're *your* generation," Shaun stressed.

"And that scares me the most. They're going to need psychiatrists some day, and they won't have a clue how to talk about their innermost feelings."

"You have a smart one here, Madeline."

She winked at the cybergigolo. A light flashed from behind us.

"I heard there was a shortage of psychiatrists," said Connor. He came forward and lowered his camera.

"Really?" I stressed.

"The public won't need psychiatrists," Shaun added. "As long as they learn the art of love, they'll connect."

I stepped forward and studied the three icons, breathing in their savoir faire. "So really, who are you? How did you become so famous that people throw lavish parties in your honor?"

"We're the ones with the digital megaphone," Connor said. "But it didn't happen overnight." Click. That was a photo I wasn't looking forward to seeing. "We worked hard at it, and somehow, we got noticed more than the others."

"Worked at what, exactly?"

"Tayler, sixty years ago, people thought email was a miracle. They'd share videos and jokes with select friends before they found they had a voice. A voice that could spread to hundreds, perhaps thousands of people on old social media platforms. They talked about their lives to anyone who was willing to listen."

"You haven't answered my question."

"He always avoids questions when he's on one of his famous rants," said Shaun.

Connor smirked. "But the downside is that everyone's staying at home more," he continued.

I gestured to the spectacle of leather, lace, and flesh around us.

"Okay, at least these people have gone out for the night. But for what? Just to be seen in the right circles."

"So why did *you* come out tonight?" asked my date.

"I was curious. Plus I needed a night out. The only invitation I had this evening was an online karaoke hookup. A work colleague wanted me to log on as she couldn't, but I had to tell her I don't own a computer. Hell, a century ago, people went out for sing-alongs. Now everyone seems to spend their evenings connecting with strangers."

"You sound bitter." Madeline seemed genuinely concerned.

"No, just lost."

"What are you lost about?" Connor asked.

"A lot of things."

"Like what?"

The teenage girls in nighties sniffed their share of powder from the coffee table.

"Those kids for example. Why are they here except to be seen? And when did all this start? Could you imagine if schools still existed? Their lives would be filled with ideas and curiosity or something worthwhile."

My audience seemed perplexed. "Schools still exist," said Madeline Q.

"But only online. Do you realize I was the last generation to be taught in a real school? Well, at least in my early years. By the time I was twelve, I had to log on, so my family moved to a cheaper neighborhood. They worked online, so it didn't matter where they lived. But I missed having my friends around me. We talked about kid stuff. Played with anything we could get our hands on. Made our own entertainment. Did all sorts of things preteens did. After that, life was solo."

"Are you lonely?" Madeline's kind tone reminded me of my fourth-grade teacher. Shaun gazed at her like a suspicious husband.

"Do you want more followers, Tayler?" Connor asked.

"No. I just want to connect with someone the way I did before Social Media Central became the soul-eating monster in everyone's lives."

Before I knew what was happening, Madeline clutched me against her chest. The blissful odors of light perspiration, laundered cotton, and watermelon perfume immersed me. I traced a path down her back with my fingertips. I shuddered, surprising myself. She leaned back to share a tender smile before letting me go and taking my hand.

"I think our girl's smitten," said Connor.

"Yes, not a sight you see every day," Shaun agreed. "Are you about to lead him astray?"

She raised a brow. "No, I'm just taking a leaf from *your* book."

# Four

"COFFEE?" I ASKED. I was at Madeline's bedroom door holding a tray with two cups and a pot I had brewed. "I found your plunger next to the coffee beans. Oh, and I found teabags if you prefer tea instead."

"Coffee is fine, darling."

But I didn't move from my spot. Behind her, the rich plum-colored wall screamed for attention. The shade was less severe the evening before, as was the industrial metallic bed-head, which curved like the lower half of a yin-and-yang symbol. She rested in the center of it, commanding this master bedroom as Cleopatra would've mastered her own.

"I wasn't sure you'd be awake yet," I said. "But now that I see you are, I'm surprised you're not on a mobile screen." I strolled in.

"There's time for work and there's time for play."

I presented the tray to her. "Milk? Sugar?"

She sat up, taking one of the cups. "Black is fine."

Her nipples were larger than dollar coins and as red as her flawless hair. She sipped and then examined her coffee, swirling the cup as if her fortune could be read by the ripples on its surface.

"You like watching me, don't you?" she said, analyzing me like a child with a new toy.

"Sorry, I didn't mean to stare."

"No, I like it. It's a fresh change from someone just getting to know me to boost their social media standing."

I looked around the room. "There's no hidden cameras here, are there? I mean, we're not on twenty-four-hour webcam, are we?"

"I leave naked theatrics to Shaun."

"I didn't realize he had sex on camera."

"No, of course he doesn't. He just blogs about his exploits and charges more if people want to read the hidden section on his profile." She had a puppy-dog gaze. "You can sit next to me if you want, Tayler."

"Sorry, I should learn to relax."

"And stop apologizing."

I put down the tray, took my coffee, and lay next to her. In front of me, two framed posters, almost the height of the wall, made bold statements with jagged lines and block shapes. In the corner, a tall wooden lamp with a smooth sandpapered surface, resembled the female form.

"How do you pay for all this?"

She bit her bottom lip.

"Sorry, am I being too forward?"

"I told you, stop apologizing." She scanned her room. "How do *you* think I pay for all this?"

"Well, I can't imagine people interested in fashion would pay more for a hidden online section."

"Tayler, you are too sweet. You really have no idea how famous Connor, Shaun, and I are." I slumped. She put her finger under my chin and pressed up, raising my head. "People pay for my *Madeline Q Predicts* secret blog. Well, it's not that secret as there's a big ad for it on my home page, but they're willing to subscribe."

"How much?"

"A hundred dollars a month."

Her finger kept my jaw from dropping. "And what do you publish on the secret blog?"

She picked up a palm-sized remote and pointed it at one of the oversized artworks. In a blink, images of her in outlandish fashions replaced the drawing.

"Which one do you want to look at?"

"You look like an ostrich in that one." I pointed. "Enlarge it."

She scowled as the picture filled the frame. Deep green feathers poured from her neck as she gave a face that would harden concrete. The rest of the dress was wrapped tightly above her knees, while a colossal bonnet in the same emerald shade, rested on her head.

"I wanted to wear black thick-framed glasses for this outfit, but the designer wouldn't hear of it. He's a Nazi when it comes to his creations. You're not impressed, are you, Tayler?"

"How did you know, Ms. Q?"

"By your smirk." She chuckled. "And call me Madi, please."

"But you told me to call you—"

She ruffled my hair. "Madi will be fine. It will be nice to hear my name said without pretention. Stop smirking. Pretention is my image."

"Weird hats and plucked birds seem to be your image."

She shook her head. "What are you doing today, Tayler?"

"Going to work."

"Take the day off. Come with me to a fashion show. Connor and Shaun will be there."

"Your life is a fairy tale."

"And yours could be too." She kissed me. Long. Lingering. Precious.

"How could I say no to those lips?"

"You're such a smoothie, in a cute nerdy kind of way."

I peered back at the image from her *Madeline Q Predicts* page. "So, this is fashion?"

"It will be by next season."

"And am I meeting the creator of the bird dress today?"

"The government never finances—" She bit her bottom lip again.

"What's the government got to do with this?"

"It's the name of the fashion designer."

"Which one?"

"Which one what?"

"The one responsible for today's social outing or the one responsible for making an ostrich bald?"

She pointed to her image. "The one who's dictating the look this spring."

SNAP! WE HARDLY stepped outside Madeline's door, and already a team of groupies were taking her picture. Then a guy took *my* image.

"So what are you?" he said.

"Huh?"

"Are you a blogger, a post jockey, a quick phrase, a filmmaker, a photographer, or a lover?"

"I bet he's a lover," said a grinning teenager.

"He can't be," said her friend. "Madeline Q doesn't shop online. Isn't that true, Ms. Q?"

"That's true," my celebrity one-night stand said. "I'm glad to see you're a well-read woman."

I clenched my lips tight.

"So, which are you?" asked an older gent near the back. He folded his arms, seemingly more to keep warm than to make a statement.

"He's all of them and none of them." She winked at me.

"Is he your boyfriend, Madeline Q?"

"Why? Are you jealous?"

"Never take love too lightly," the older gent said. "In an age of electronic social desperation, he may be the only thing worth coming back to."

I smiled to myself.

"Weirdo," jibed one of the teenagers.

"Listen to this man," I said. "You don't want to masturbate in front of a screen all your life."

"He's right," the man continued. "You know our population is shrinking. Shit, ten percent of the last generation died virgins."

"Ew!" shrieked the teen. "I don't want to get a disease."

"Who told you that, you silly girl?"

"I read it online."

"Now, now," said Madi. "My front door is not a place for debate or name-calling."

A murmur ran through the small crowd. The elder pulled out his mobile screen. The lens in his small device extended as he pointed it at me.

"What's your name?"

Madi placed her arm around my shoulder and declared, "His name is Tayler."

The others pronounced my name, took extra shots, and uploaded.

# Five

BEFORE WE ARRIVED at the fashion event, we detoured to Connor's apartment. But on the way, I'd felt both uneasy and proud when I was out in the street. Why? People I didn't know knew my name. They'd point or pull out their small screens and capture my stance as I walked with Madi.

Some looked like bodies whose spirits were taken as payment in a satanic deal, their eyes hungry for a taste of what I had. But they couldn't reach me without pointing. No way to simply greet me and strike up a conversation. Their speech was easier when expressed in keystrokes.

And the titanic glass structures, a symbol of a city that believed in its own majesty, looked down upon these scattered beings and wished to hear them laugh and converse. These dejected buildings once teemed with life before more and more work was done online. So people moved out in search of cheaper real estate, leaving those left behind as empty as Astra City itself.

And although I'd never felt their particular brand of emptiness, I did from time to time feel my own distinct version of lonely. Thankfully, not today. For today, it seemed cotton candy had wrapped my heart. From this moment, my voice would transmit sugar-coated thoughts that didn't rot the minds of the mainstream, if they were ready to listen. And I'd skate along in lollypop shoes or glide on chocolate wings. White chocolate, of course.

I was not typical of my peers, but then again, I wasn't in the league of the Social Media Central giants. I was that awkward boy, good-looking enough, but as self-aware as someone with a pimple in plain sight. People scrutinized me when we met, and even when I took the lead in making my presence felt, I quickly retreated in my cocoon once they took over our exchange. Did it worry me? Nah. I was used to being somewhere in between. I'd learned to be there.

As we entered Connor's flat, I was relieved he didn't sport a camera. Then I was swept away by the vast space of his pad, my oohs and aahs echoing in his warehouse conversion. Huge portrait photos hung on every inch of wall. A kitchen that would be the pride of any meticulous carpenter was showcased proudly in the center. The floorboards creaked a little, making me stop to notice the fatherly scent of wood polish. Spherical metal lights of differing size floated like planets. To my left stood several manikins wearing loud shirts and one in a classic black dress.

"So these are the costumes?" Madeline inquired.

"This *Nineteen-Sixties Go Mad* fashion extravaganza will be the talk of the stratosphere this evening," Connor replied.

"I like my little black dress."

"Your red hair will flame against the fabric," I said.

She caressed my head. "You know what, Tayler? I'm glad you're here."

Madi slipped her dress from its manikin and casually made her way to a bedroom. Connor watched her like a protective brother. We took off our shirts and started buttoning up our paisley tops.

"So the government sends the party outfits here," I noted.

"Oh, Madeline told you about the government?"

"Yeah. It seems no expense is spared." I brushed my beard against the silk collar.

"True. Look at how much money was spent on the Eros party. Leather. Lace. All the gold-and-black furniture and fittings."

"The apartment was decorated for the event?"

"Yes, the owner put in an application to host, and the government paid the bill."

I stopped rolling up my sleeve. "Why pay that expense?"

"Tayler, the masses need to daydream."

"Uh-huh."

"And we are the ones sparking their desires."

"But why?"

"Well, government is power, but when no one is listening to the government's message because they're too wrapped up sharing their top-ten tunes for that month or commenting on whether Aunt Tabitha should make a red velvet or sponge cake, the government has to find new ways to talk to its people."

"Fascinating."

"How much did Madeline tell you?"

The bedroom door opened. My heart sank in fear she'd overheard us, but she called out to see if he had a jacket to go with the dress.

"No," Connor called back. "But there's a mink coat in the wardrobe. It's mine, but it could work on you."

She shut the door.

"Well, what I still don't understand is how people following your lifestyle gives the government its voice?"

"That's right. You don't really go online do you, Tayler? In the comments posted in response to my photos, or Shaun or Madeline's blogs, are the streams of thought from society. And within their comments are our responses. Our positive reactions to policies or what passes for policy and whatever else we've been told to say through Social Media Central."

"But if you're making political observation on your social media, surely there's been debate."

"Not as much as you'd think, Tayler. Plus we have the power to delete unwanted comments."

"Really? Why you guys?"

"Well, we were chosen specifically."

"Why?"

"People took more notice of us than of what the government had to say."

"So the government finances your elaborate lifestyles so you stay on top of the social media pile."

"Kind of. They created our elaborate lifestyles to keep us on top of the social media pile, once they realized the people were listening to our voice."

"What do you think?" Madi called from the bedroom. She modeled her ensemble.

"Lose the coat," Connor yelled.

I nodded.

"I thought the same," she said and closed the door.

"Even I could see it was a mismatch," I said.

"Why are you frowning?"

"I've just had that sinking feeling that without the government's help, she'd be just another plain-Jane."

"Trust me, Tayler, they keep her in touch with the best designers."

"Bare shoulders are in again," Madi said. She made her way toward us like a siren ready to take the town. "Besides, it's not really that cold this afternoon."

She took my hand and headed for the front door as Connor scrambled for his camera.

THE SAME DOZEN models stepped down the catwalk on high rotation, parading everything from floral prints to outfits resembling rejects from my granny's quilt-making days. A band that looked like they'd rather be surfing played instrumentals for the modest-sized crowd. And every dress, jacket, and skirt was photographed by my new friend, Connor.

Afterward, I stood sipping champagne with Shaun and Madi, as Connor succeeded in getting most of the guests to look up from their mobile screens just long enough to snap them.

"Apparently, the audience has reached twelve million," Madi said.

"What are you talking about?" I asked. "There's only about seventy here."

"It's being streamed through Social Media Central," Shaun said.

"Oh, that's why most people are watching it on their devices, rather than experiencing it in reality," I said. "I didn't think they were really interested in hundred-year-old fashion."

"Look at them. They're checking if the video cameras caught them."

I surveyed the room. Thin black strips of smoked glass had been placed against every corner. Dark snow globes hung from different parts of the ceiling. Within these were the new streamlined lenses that recorded everything. AV Enterprises, the company I worked for, designed them.

"How long do we need to stick around?" I asked.

Madi smiled. "Bored already?"

"Tayler, we all get bored at these events more than we admit to," said Shaun. "But it's our duty to enjoy ourselves." My date looked at him like he'd just exposed his private parts. "Madeline, Tayler knows about our affiliation with the government. Come to think of it, you know he knows about our affiliation with the government. Connor mentioned that you already told him."

Her eyes met mine. "Did I?"

"Not in so many words, but I can read between the lines."

She ruffled my hair. "You are a very smart man. What else did you and Connor talk about?"

"About how the government made all your stars shine."

"Tayler," yelled a plump man who was waddling our way. He had matched his toupee with fake sideburns, which went with his fake fur waistcoat.

"Hi," I said. "How are you?"

"Don't pretend you know me. You don't. But I know you. I'm a fan."

"Of me?"

"Yes, Tayler. Of you!"

"Oh."

It was hard to suppress my gleeful grin until he planted a sloppy kiss on my cheek. Shaun and Madi laughed.

"Manners, please," my admirer reprimanded. "Tayler is a flower in bloom. He's a star on the rise. He's a rocket shooting into space." The man's eyebrows raised on his last sentence. He turned to Madi with his mobile device in his hand. "Could you please take our picture?"

"Sure thing, lover boy. Say cheese."

The evidence was taken. A middle-aged man took a selfie with me. Being recognized was one thing, but publicly broadcasting this type of person as my fan-base was another. *When did I become so shallow?*

My date handed his screen back before blowing me a kiss. Then both she and Shaun crept away like thieves in a silent movie.

"So tell me, Tayler, how did you meet Madeline Q?"

"Ms. Q and I met in a park."

"Hmm, that hasn't been reported." He swiped his small screen and typed in the information. "Go on. Who said what to whom first?"

"Why are you taking an interest in me, err…?"

"Patrick."

"Huh?"

"My name is Patrick, as in 'Why are you taking an interest in me, Patrick?'"

"Hello, Patrick. Why are you taking an interest in me?"

"Sweetheart, you've broken in. You're one of the pack now, and there'll be no turning back." His fingers walked up my arm. "And everyone here will want a part of you."

"But why? Seriously?"

"Seriously? You need to ask?"

"Yes I do. Why?"

"You are royalty, Tayler. Why else would I be stepping into your spotlight and reporting on things that aren't known yet?"

"But what about finding success your own way? Through your own means."

His finger danced on his screen once more. "So, who spoke first, you or Madeline Q?"

# Six

"ARE WE A couple?" I asked.

Madeline still retained elegance sitting naked on the mattress on my floor. "I'm here, aren't I?"

"But I could be just your plaything."

"Tayler, I'm not rushing things, but that doesn't mean I'm not interested. Hey, we just had sex on two consecutive days."

It was the evening of the sixties fashion parade, and we had stopped off at my bachelor pad. I watched her face when we first strolled in. She didn't wince at my lack of furniture. She didn't faint when she saw my unmade mattress. She didn't mention a designer overhaul. She simply clutched my shirt collar and pulled me toward her lips.

And now we sat on my makeshift bed. Another layer of her mystique seemed to have slipped away as I noted her kinder expression. Her flowing red hair didn't dazzle me anymore, but her tasty breasts, peeking through the strands, still did. My tongue desired another sample before I slid into her adoring space. A place of true art that no designer could enhance.

But we were talking. In my mind, I was telling my cock not to stir. I wanted this conversation with her. Not with Madeline Q, but with *her*.

"I excite you," she noted.

"Ignore my penis. I really want us to talk."

"Talk about what, Tayler? I've already told you I like you. And from what I can see between your legs, I know you like me."

I exhaled loudly as I looked away, shutting my eyes at the same time. "Madi, tell me about yourself."

She clutched my cock. "Are you sure you want to talk?"

"Yes. If you don't mind, could you please let go?"

She did.

"It will still be there when we need it."

"My dear metrosexual lover, what do you want to talk about?"

"Madi, I've spent more time with you than with Shaun and Connor, and even though they're still strangers, I feel I know them better. So tell me about you. Tell me about your life before Madeline Q."

"What do you want to know?"

"Just pick a point and start."

She eased her knees to her breasts and wrapped her arms around her legs. "Any point in my life? Hmm. I came to Astra City when I was twenty-three. Like all of us in our twenties, I wanted to find myself or reinvent myself, whichever came first." She smirked.

"But why did you leave home?"

"Tayler, let's leave that part of the story for another day. For now, just know I wanted to expand my horizons." She looked up to the ceiling. "To be honest, there's no one from my first years here I still see. I partied a lot but never connected with anyone on a deeper level. That was before I met Connor."

"Really? Connor? You've known him for that long?"

"Yep. I saw him at a party. He was standing by himself against the wall, studying people like he was casting them for a film. And this sounds silly now, but I didn't realize he was homosexual."

"Were you attracted to him?"

"A little. He didn't wear his trademark sunglasses in those days, so his lashes stood out."

I raised a brow.

"Seriously, Connor has sexy eyelashes. Nice auburn eyes too, but his eyelashes are a treat."

"So you went up to him?"

"I went up to him and said the most ridiculous line." She paused, looking at me as if she was confessing. "I said, *Are you in the market for adventure?* He replied, *Only if you're a drag queen.* And that, lover boy, was the start of a beautiful friendship."

"You're not telling me much, Madi."

"I'm just collecting my thoughts. To state the obvious, we got drunk that night. He was in a relationship, and although his boyfriend wasn't there, a friend of his boyfriend was throwing the party. If you ask me, I think he was a bit lost without his better half."

"Go on."

"Sadly, Connor and his man had a big row a few days after. Apparently, it was the biggest row they ever had."

"Madi, you're not really talking about yourself."

"Well, I am. Sort of. You see, Connor was my lifeline. He knew people, but he seemed distant from them. When we went out together, we were the ones filling up everyone's drinks and getting them to talk to each other. We were the ones on the dance floor first, making fools of ourselves before others would join us. He brought out something in me, and I brought out something in him."

"Excuse me for interrupting, but I don't see you both acting like that now."

"Fame does weird things to people, Tayler." She laughed. "This is the sort of conversation people have at bars with overpriced cocktails in their hands."

"Those that can afford cocktails."

"What was I saying, lover?"

"You were saying how fame does weird things to people."

"Yes, it does. You sneak back inside your skin. It's the only safe way to handle the obsessed." She placed her hand on my shoulder. "Tayler, I can read your expression, and yes, your first fan earlier this afternoon was loud and painful, but trust me, other people at that party were asking about you. They wanted to know everything there was to know about you. You're the newbie on the block." Her hand moved away. "Your face lights up when you smile. Some cute fan is going to fall in love with that smile."

"When I fall in love, you'll be the first to know."

"One of us is bound to say I love you. That scares me a little."

"When was your last boyfriend?"

"Not long before I moved to the city."

"Raw nerve?"

"Wait until we're in a bar with overpriced drinks. And do me a favor. Please don't ask Connor about my last boyfriend. I want you to hear about him from me."

SHORTLY AFTER OUR heart-to-heart on my mattress, it was time for passion before a quick visit to Connor's to change into our preselected outfits for that evening's function.

"It's classy yet understated," I said.

"It's you," Madi said.

"I agree," Connor added. "I don't think it's what you normally wear, but boy, you're making it sing."

I twirled in front of Connor's full-length mirror several times, like my landlady must have before each cyberdate. The black jeans clutched my ass so tight I was surprised I could still walk. And the turtleneck highlighted the thick frames of my glasses, making me yearn to parade down the catwalk myself. Yes, tonight I was worthy of Madeline Q's affection.

And yet, as these thoughts entered my head while still spinning around in front of my reflection and falling deeper in love with myself, an imaginary angel sat on my shoulder telling me to come down from the clouds.

"Are we ready?" Connor said.

"I don't think I want to leave this mirror."

"Cinderella, your ensemble will turn back to rags if we don't venture outside my apartment soon."

Madi held my hand. "Tayler, you're looking mighty delicious."

"Delicious?"

"Even I'd eat you," Connor said.

With my date in a smart suit and loose tie and Connor donning a fawn jacket and pants, we headed for a small bookstore only two blocks down the road.

"DESIGNER MALE DRAG," Shaun said to Madi. She grabbed her tie and swung it around like a tassel.

"I may be in a suit, but I'm still more woman than you can handle."

"Ouch."

A small circle of groupies photographed us. A short-haired woman in stilettos sharp enough to pierce flesh, strolled toward our love blogger, gracefully edging through our fans. She held her hand out, and Shaun kept his attention on her. He took her hand and shook it steadily.

"Felicity," she said.

"Shaun."

"I know. I bet you're used to women coming up to you." More flashes from the mobile screens. Felicity shut her eyes and shook her head. "Children, can't you go and play outside? This is a bookstore for heaven's sake. We're trying to have a small intimate affair for grown-ups."

"Yes. Listen to that woman. Listen and learn." I couldn't see who said this, as the small pond of photo-taking piranhas was blocking my view. But it was definitely a male voice, close to my own age.

"Do you know who these people are?" screamed a girl whose voice nearly made my ears bleed.

"Yes, I do, but that doesn't mean you need to harass them."

I could see him now. He stood against the bookcase containing the volumes for sale. His bushy hair flopped over his lined forehead like he had just climbed out of bed. He hadn't shaved for a few days, and his shirt looked like it was ironed by a nearsighted maid. He smiled at me. I was already smiling at him.

"We can behave," said a scrawny male. He lowered his small screen. "It's just that this is the first time I've seen Connor, Shaun, Madeline Q, or Tayler in person. They don't usually do these types of events."

"You make us sound uncultured," Shaun remarked.

"Well, you usually do the glamour stuff. You don't hang around in our circles."

"Speak for yourself," shrieked the annoying girl. "I was at the Eros party. Cost me a fortune to attend. But I guess if I want to be noticed, fame comes at a price."

She lurched forward and licked me on the cheek. I recoiled like a camper who'd been bitten by a snake. Felicity grabbed the disgusting creature and escorted her out the door. Connor handed me his handkerchief.

Felicity then asked if anyone else was more interested in the Social Media Socialites than Mike's book launch. The author held up his novel before using it to gesture to the empty chairs in the first row. Our fans looked to us as we also gestured toward the front. They begrudgingly ambled to the seats. We stayed on our feet at the back.

"SHAUN, I OWN this bookstore," Felicity whispered. "I'm glad you're here, but boy, your fans are hard to take."

"I'm afraid it comes with the territory," he replied.

They were snapping and uploading our pictures, but not at the frenetic pace we were used to. They were trying to fit in, yet with so few photos being taken, each flash was as noticeable as a hungry mosquito.

"Look at them," the store owner continued. "Don't they have something better to do?"

"We *are* their something-better-to-do." Shaun and Felicity watched the handful of circling devotees.

"They're like vultures waiting to step into the limelight once your fame expires."

"That's an interesting analogy," Connor said. "And yet my job is to hold a mirror to them with my own camera." He paused momentarily for a shot. "So am I as bad, Felicity?"

"Your photos are art. You make a statement, an essay if you like, on your profile page. You capture your own fame through the eyes of the wannabes."

"I'm flattered."

"And what about you, Tayler?"

"What about me?"

"You're new to this. The others must be used to this playground of fools. How do you view them?"

Madi, who had been protectively clutching onto me from behind, let go, leaving me to stand free.

"It's weird, but I'm not jaded yet."

"You're far from jaded," Connor interrupted. "You're still the kid in the candy store. Don't look at me like that, Tayler. I'm saying it with love."

"He is," said Shaun. "Madi, Connor, and I were you once. We welcomed the attention of strangers until we realized it was all a bit strange."

"Yet you persist on fostering the fame addicts," said Felicity.

"The very fame addicts who have made your bookstore famous tonight," Madi declared. "And I don't mean to sound rude, but having us here means tomorrow, there will be a line of followers waiting to buy a book when you open those doors. And it won't matter what book they buy, as long as they can take a selfie featuring the book in your customized bag and say they shopped here."

"I can't argue with that. I wish I could, but I can't. With your help, I might be able to fill a second bookcase."

"That's why you're paying us," Connor said playfully. "To revitalize the printed word!"

"Paying us?" I asked.

"Well, Mike is paying you," said Felicity. "This was all his idea."

"Pardon me for saying this," said Connor, "but he doesn't look like he can afford us."

"Apparently, he's been saving since the initial keystroke of his first draft."

"Clever man," Madi noted.

Connor raised his camera, zoomed in, and took a portrait of a writer touching stardom. He captured various poses with Mike's new readership, all of them holding their mobile screens in front of their favorite new author and themselves. And through all of this, Mike stayed composed, like a dreaming author waiting to meet his muse in some unexplored magical realm.

Then he looked my way and tilted his head, while the potential reader trying to take a selfie with the man of the moment glared in my direction. She scrunched her lips, then took the photo anyway.

"All of you have a captive audience," said Felicity. "You should use your power to start people talking, you know, verbally. Not just by posting comments."

"Felicity, that would require our audience to think for themselves," Connor said. "LOL."

"LOL? See, that's my point. This old phrase has made a comeback, yet do we remember what it means? The Chinese use painted characters, or symbols if you like, that mean things. That's how they write. And we too started using letters as symbols. If we wanted to say something is funny, we type LOL or shoved in an emoji. Language has shrunk over many years. Real communication is needed to bring it back."

"But LOL has been around for more than half a century," Madi said.

"And does anyone remember what it means?"

We all looked to Connor.

"Don't ask me," he said. "Lots of laughter?"

"Laughing often, loudly," I said. "But that doesn't make sense. Why would you say you're laughing a lot when you throw it in now and again?"

"I thought it meant, love, only laughing," Madi confessed. "That's the context I use it in."

"It's laugh out loud," said Shaun.

"Are you sure?"

"Very sure."

"Whatever it means, you have power," said Felicity. "Shit, you have more power than the government."

"I could see myself ruling," Connor said. "I swear I'd do a better job."

"Yes, dear," Madi said. "You'd get the groupie vote. LOL."

"Don't laugh," Shaun said. "We've got enough groupies to vote in any one of us. We could simply mention it in a blog and they'd comply."

Only two of our fans were in the bookstore now, still desperately taking countless shots of a book launch that was nearing its end.

"But Felicity's right about one thing," said Mike. He strolled toward us with one of the fans following close behind.

"What's Felicity right about?" I asked.

"You could harness your power for good."

"How?"

The others exchanged glances, yet I didn't know why.

"Family members are growing up without ever really knowing each other."

"But that's true of everyone I know. And the older I get, the less I talk to my *own* family."

He pulled his device from his jean pocket and waved it in the air. "I have my contacts in here. Originally, I had my parents and my closest friends. Eventually, I stopped calling them because I could see what they were up to through their posts. Then new people contacted me, and I added them to my phone. I started to get excited seeing what they were up to, yet I'd never met or spoken to them face to face."

"That's normal," said Madi. "That's why they call it Social Media Central."

"Is it normal, really? Is it normal that people I actually knew face to face are as relevant as people I've never met? And that I hardly call those people I know well? Even when I do, the conversation is awkward. My own dad and I don't speak anymore. The need is gone. If I feel the urge to see what he's up to, I can find out on SMC."

"But you still have him in your contact list. It's up to you to make the effort."

"No, Madi, I see his point," I said. "The device holds his contacts close to his heart, if you like, so for most people, that's enough. They're always with them, even if they don't speak. So everyone on that list is now an acquaintance."

"An acquaintance?" asked the fan who'd joined us.

"It's an old word for people that you know but don't know well enough to be your friend."

"But everyone is a friend."

"No, they aren't." I turned to Mike, ignoring her confusion. "Why don't you talk to your dad?"

"Because his world is all about this." Again he waved his device above him. "And I have better ways to seek validation than to use Social Media Central."

"I hear you loud and clear, Mike. My parents fell away a long time ago. All former living beings in their world have fallen to acquaintance level, and the newbies have risen to the same relevance, making them all safe and controllable."

"So if families aren't talking to each other, what can we do?" Connor asked.

Mike grabbed a copy of his book from a shelf. "Get them to communicate through this!"

"You're an opportunist, Mike," said Madi. "Any excuse to get us to promote your writing."

"That's not what I meant. As social media socialites, you can create a new trend where someone suggests a book to their father, their sister or whoever, which sheds light on their relationship. For example, it could be a novel about lost childhood, and a girl who felt her parents were absent as she grew up might suggest it to her mother, hoping to start a conversation. Or it may be a comedy that someone suggests to a friend that they're not close to anymore, but they have the same sense of humor. It's a way of sharing thoughts and ideas with people they want to reconnect with. Or maybe just connect with for the first time."

"I like that idea," I said. "But no one really reads anything longer than a blog post anymore."

Felicity gestured to the fifty or so books on her shelves.

"Okay, some do," I said. "But not the audience that follows us. Yet everyone has several favorite movies."

"I like the way you think," said Mike. "They suggest a film for someone else to watch that is dear to the person suggesting it. Then they talk about it afterward, hopefully on a personal level. Everyone's been touched by cinema. What would you suggest I watch if I wanted to know you better, Tayler?"

"I have embarrassing tastes, Mike."

"Hey, I have a weird love of silent movies."

"Okay, that makes my love of century-old cinema seem normal."

"So what would you pick?" he asked.

"Something obscure, like *Head* featuring a manufactured pop band."

"Aren't they all manufactured these days?"

I shrugged.

"Why that film?"

"It's surreal and esoteric."

"And what would that tell me about you, Tayler?" The others leaned forward. "Are you surreal and esoteric?"

"I guess so."

"No, I don't think you are. I think it means you're one of a kind, Tayler, and in today's world, that's rare."

"Thank you, Mike."

He briefly studied my new associates, scanning them collectively from head to toe. "Yes my friend, you're an original. Now, promise me you won't end up a carbon copy."

# Seven

MY PERSONAL AUTOPILOT mode slipped into gear the next morning. I had no choice. It was a workday. I immersed myself in water trying to wash away my sleep. My private rainfall couldn't knock me out of zombie state. I lathered, taking in the sandalwood scent, and my eyelids eventually stayed open.

The company bus picked me up. My colleagues hooked into Social Media Central, or perhaps to be more accurate, SMC hooked *them* in. I drifted off on a different page.

The stage actors that took residence in my mind invited countless female extras to star in my daydreams. They all yearned for countless selfies in various stages of undress and then posted their titillating stories on Tayler Net. My numerous romances would be documented with glowing praise. My techniques would be celebrated. Others would try, then admire my wisdom in the art of love. *Where is my head at?* But still, it was nice to dream.

I stepped off the bus and into AV Enterprises, following my soulless work colleagues through the steel building. We plodded on the polished concrete, taking left or right turns as we arrived at our individual offices. My computer greeted me by name before it began its daily ritual of showing me the day's duties.

That day, it did something different, though. It listed my obligations in relation to their importance, then presented me with the spreadsheet for my first task. It had decided the order of my chores. I carefully checked the requests and provided quotes. The morning wore on.

At my customary break at exactly quarter to eleven, my spreadsheet shrunk on my screen, and a video showed us the latest developments at AV Enterprises. It had been the same presentation of surveillance cameras, hidden microphones, projection devices, and exotic small-screens for the past week. I stood, stretching my arms above my head before pushing my left palm gently against the fingertips of my right hand, all for the sake of avoiding nasty computer pains.

The show-and-tell presentation finished, so I sat back at my desk. The spreadsheet returned. I stared at it, like it was a monster I had to outsmart. I tapped my keyboard, but eventually I just typed the same letter over and over again. The font turned disciplinary red. My minor act of rebellion made me smile.

For the next five minutes, I entered the correct quotes, gradually moving my eyes closer and closer to the screen. My finger missed the spacebar. It missed it a second time, then a third. I stood and stretched again. I needed air. I opened my door.

I walked down the hall of the dead. Fingers tapped their keyboards. Voices cursed their mistakes. Bodies slumped in their chairs. Of course, I couldn't see any of this behind all the closed offices, but it's what played out with that cast in my mind.

Then I heard the familiar robotic voice of my computer's ringtone call my name. I rushed back to my desk and clicked the answer icon on my screen.

"You're not going to be happy with us."

"Why?" I asked the voice I didn't recognize coming from my designer external speaker.

"They sound perfect. Those little buggers can produce an earthquake if they had to. But we can't get the projections to work."

"Earthquake?"

"Yeah. They have amazing surround sound, shooting audio in all directions. We played police sirens through them, and our neighborhood left their cocoons to see what was going on. Mayhem everywhere! People I'd never seen in the months I've lived here were looking up and down the street for the noise. So, for sound, these buggers are great."

"Who is this?"

"What do you mean who is this?" An image of my caller appeared on my screen. Two sparkling studs sat on his earlobes. An outline of a beard, as if shaded with a pencil, highlighted his jaw, with hairs just as short shaping the top of his latte-toned head. His face alone had enough appeal to stop all speech. And his steel blue eyes darted life into my dull office. "You're younger than I expected," he said.

"No one's said that to me before."

He smiled an infectious smile. "Anyway, we just can't get the light projections to work. Well, they work, but the animation bit doesn't."

"Sorry, I still don't know who you are."

"I'm Hendrix. You know, from the private messages."

I shook my head. "I think you have me mixed up with someone else."

"You're Tyler, aren't you? That's who you're supposed to be."

"No, I'm Tayler. Tyler is way above me in management circles. Our damned automated receptionist sometimes sends his calls to me."

"Oh." His lips formed this word as if he was about to blow a smoke ring.

"So, when you said Tyler, the software mistook it for Tayler. That's why you've been put through to me. I can transfer you to Tyler if you like."

He looked away as if someone else was in the room. "Yes, please."

Even without a smile, something lifted him above the pack. He was more self-assured, even in this moment of uncertainty, than anyone I'd ever encountered in Astra City.

"Okay then," I said.

I transferred the call. He never thanked me or faced his webcam again as his image left my screen. And then I felt a sinking feeling in the pit of my gut that had no reason to be there. My work screen flashed a large exclamation mark at me, waiting for a keystroke. I laughed at it, not knowing why. I stood and stepped outside my office.

Logic dictates I should have been working out what audio device Hendrix had tested. Nothing that sounded anything like it appeared in our video of the latest products. Instead, I kept thinking about his face. The faultless line of his cheekbones. Skin that showed no sign of a blemish. And not a worry line in sight. No one in Astra City looked that perfect.

"Tayler!" I turned toward the shrill voice. "Tayler, what are you doing out here?"

My plump boss and his saggy-eyed offsider scrutinized me like I was a criminal.

"You heard our manager. Why aren't you in your office?"

"There's a problem with my computer."

"What kind of problem?"

"Sometimes the screen flickers on and off."

"Let's take a look." He marched me back to my desk while my morbid manager walked away. "Show me," he commanded.

"It's spasmodic. You can see its working now, but it kept shutting off."

"Type."

I sat and tapped the keyboard. The exclamation mark disappeared.

"If it happens again, use our internal messaging system to contact me."

"But if the screen goes black again, how can I use the internal messaging system?"

"Yell for me down the hallway. I'll hear you." He strode out the door.

My computer flashed brightly three times. Like a boat heading for disaster, I sailed toward the light. The spreadsheet returned. I punched in the numbers.

As the last quote entered its cell, the list of figures shrunk and my itemized list of daily correspondence filled the screen. The first one had a curious heading. I clicked it open. My boss sent me a note, a feat rarer than virgin births.

In plain English with no rounded edges, he decided that as of tomorrow, I would do my job from home. Office space was needed for new recruits and some of the staff were quite capable of doing their jobs from their home computers. He highlighted the benefits of working this way. The company would save on transport costs, which was an odd statement for an industry that regularly made huge profits. The email pointed out that as home workers, we could attend to our pets and save money on lunches. I wasn't sure how, but I couldn't be bothered questioning.

I was supposed to take a picture of the screen displaying my unique username and password, and log onto the AV Enterprises Social Media Central page where I'd be taken to a private area to perform my office duties. Two things were wrong with this request. One, my device didn't take photos. Two, I had no computer at home.

Instead, I replied, "whatever," sending a copy to the second-in-command and also to Tyler. I felt relief as I typed his name. A quiet dispatch to show I was no fool.

I left my prison and wandered outside. My feet took me home where more dreams of half-naked nymphs were waiting.

# Eight

NOT HAVING A job wasn't a problem for too long as two weeks later, my financial prayers were answered. I was on the payroll of the government. Discreet sums were deposited into my bank account daily, while Madi, Connor, Shaun, and I kept a busy social schedule. And the best part was, I didn't need a Social Media Central profile. I was a celebrity by association.

On my first day off, I slept in. It felt amazing. Somewhere in my psyche, that loud little man who'd normally shake me out of slumber at 6:00 a.m., caught up on his own rest. Both of us found inner peace. My cloud-like pillows eased my dreams through blissful scenarios where drama was not an option. And my kindhearted mattress kept me afloat on a sea of calm.

I finally woke several hours before the day's adventure. Madi was to star in a big-budget ad, streaming live from a location I'd never heard of. Connor and I were part of the shoot, but until our individual cars picked us up, we had no idea what we were supposed to promote. I found a script in the back seat and read through my lines, not really noticing where I was being taken to.

The vehicle jolted to a stop. I bounced with it, nearly dropping my script. A brick building, rare for Astra City, towered above me. My friends were already waiting inside.

"Does he really think this will work?" Connor asked. He was strolling around the enormous space, waving his script in the air while shaking his head at the art direction.

A water fountain bubbled away proudly in the center of the room. This was, in fact, the first time I'd seen one that actually worked. A huge burgundy curtain hung just behind it, confusing me. *Is this meant to be an indoor scene or an outdoor one?* A reclining poolside chair was to the left of the water feature, complete with a side table. Sunglasses and a state-of-the-art screen lay on top of the table. *So what is the meaning of the curtain?*

I glanced at my lines but not for long. A crew wheeled in three large video cameras, stamped with the AV Enterprises logo, followed by a tall, flouncy man who clapped his hands three times to get our attention.

"Are you ready for rehearsal?"

"Do the lines have to be word perfect?" I asked.

"Tayler, darling, step onto the set."

I stumbled to the front of the fountain.

"Roll."

My lines appeared on an angular glass plate positioned in front of the middle camera, magically suspended and waiting for me to read them.

"Wow. How did you do that?"

"Ancient technology. Now, your words are in white, Tayler. Madeline, dear, yours are in yellow, and Connor, sweetheart, look out for the pink letters."

A horde of twenty-something men and women made their way through the front entrance.

"I'm glad you're here, guys," said the flouncy man to the troop. "You obviously know Madeline Q, Connor, and the delightfully delicious Tayler."

We lifted our chins and presented our trademark smiles. Screens came out. Photos were snapped. Our faces returned to normal.

"Now you lot, practice your dance steps on the other side of the curtain. We need to rehearse lines on this side. So go as far as you can toward that back wall. We go live in ninety minutes." He spun around. "Frederick. Where is that man? Frederick?"

A spikey-haired, middle-aged guy ran through a side door. His shorts left little to the imagination, while his lanky legs carried him within yelling distance of our group.

"Makeup and wardrobe are ready," he called. "We'll only need half an hour to make them all up, so send them through when you're finished with them."

"Excellent." Frederick sprinted back into seclusion. "Now, Madeline, lounge." She strode to the chair and lay like a queen. "Connor, Tayler, get in front of the water feature." We took our places. "Roll autocue."

"All of us, everyone watching this stream, is lucky to live in Astra City." I read my white words. To my surprise, more rolled up. "No, I'm serious. Just stop and think for a minute."

"The stores are always stocked with enough ingredients for any mirror meal you decide on," said Connor. His gritty tone was hard not to notice.

"Our education is first-rate," I continued. "New lessons are being developed daily for the school-aged and those needing to catch up."

"And water." Connor's lips tightened as he spoke. "Clean water is ready on tap for the most basic of human needs. Um, who wrote this shit?"

"I know," said our director. "Just go with it. We're being paid." He peered down his nose at my girlfriend who was playing with the new small screen. "Madeline Q, it's your line, dear."

"Sorry," she said. "And what does the government expect from you? Nothing." She held the device in front of her. "Just engage with your infinite world. No need for worries. No need for dramas. Just be the star of your life on Social Media Central."

"There's no more words," I said. "Is that it? We're going live for a nanosecond?"

"Gorgeous Tayler, this is reality marketing," the director said. "You will be interrupted by those dazzling dancers while Madeline Q speaks. So flirt with them. Stick your tongue out as the cute ones go past. Do whatever feels natural. Real moments get shared on Social Media Central." He bowed his head. "And yes, Connor, I know this is all horse manure, but you're getting paid a lot of money to speak these lines."

"But the way we're supposed to talk about our leader, like he's some ancient god in the sky taking care of us," said Connor. "It just makes me mad. Seriously, water, for goodness sake. Providing clean water is a government's role. It's not like he pisses out the reservoirs himself."

"I heard it's recycled," said our director.

"I've heard that too, but still, providing water is part of any leader's duty statement."

"You're an educated man, Connor. Sadly, your public is not."

"I envy your education," I said. "In fact, I envy all three of you for having a proper education. Yet here we are all doing something plastic."

"Odd change of topic," our director noted.

"I'm sorry. It's a bee in my bonnet."

"A what?"

"Something they used to say in old movies."

"And you're about to get stung," said Connor to our director.

"No, he won't," I said. "I'll shut up."

"No, Tayler, go ahead." The eccentric man leaned forward as he spoke. "I'm interested in your opinion. We're all talking freely here."

"No, seriously. Once I begin, I'll only make myself upset."

"It's a sore topic," said Connor. "It's the story of lost childhood and wayward education." He smiled at me in an encouraging way.

"This sounds like a story I have to hear," the director declared.

"Okay. I'm just jealous because you all had teachers inspiring you from your first day at school right through to graduation. Now kids are watching instructional videos rather than seeing live teachers on their screens."

"True, I guess. I never really thought about what your generation missed out on. But you're right. I was inspired by many teachers. They encouraged me to watch longer videos, you know, the older ones. Then I read books with a couple of hundred pages, you know—"

I nodded. "The older ones."

"Yes, the older ones, with wit and charm and characters that thought. And here I am thirty years later with you and my so-called contribution to the arts."

He half smiled like a man on life support. Connor studied the room once more while Madi stayed glued to her screen.

"What's your name?" Connor asked.

"Soho. I know it's pretentious, but it's my real name."

"Why is it pretentious?" I asked.

"You precious young boy, I see your point. You're a generation who lost your education."

I lowered my head. "True. When I was twelve, it all went online. Part of the all-encompassing Social Media Central. And when I was twelve, I kept searching for Audrey." Somehow even the dancers were now silent from the back of the room. "No, she wasn't a playmate or a girl I liked. She was a teacher I had in fourth class who helped me sense the other kids. Okay, I know that sounds odd, but hear me out."

Even Madi put down her screen.

"Growing up, I always felt like I was in the background. I was unimportant, somehow. Everyone else was the star. Audrey showed me that I was the star, but just a moody one wanting attention, and unless I was happy to share that attention, nothing was going to change. So she devised games where we actually did physical things, like chase each other or chase a ball. Once we even held on a string and flew this thing into the sky."

"A kite," said Soho.

"Was it? I don't remember what it was called, but that day I finally got it. I shared me, and others shared themselves. And we talked and played and..."

Madi stood, strode toward me, and cradled me in her arms. "That's a weight off your chest, lover."

"Keep those connections, boy," Soho whispered. "You have them here, in your tribe. And you have the power to tell your fans what they're missing out on." The expansive room became as silent as a monastery. After a minute or two, Soho clapped his hands again. "Okay, Frederick. Get everyone made up!"


"OUR ONLINE IDENTITY is like a prosthetic limb," said a blond male dancer.

Connor rubbed his chin. "I've never thought about my identity like that, but you're right."

"I'm glad someone like you sees my point."

"I don't get it," said Madi.

"It's that external force that is part of us, but it's the superficial part," Connor explained.

"Is it? I consider Madeline Q as me."

I was standing in a funky tropical shirt while a fresh layer of foundation was applied to my face. I wanted to weigh in, but Connor was doing a good job voicing what I was thinking.

"But Madeline Q is not the Madeline I know. And it's definitely not the Madeline, or the Madi, that Tayler knows."

She looked to me. I nodded.

"Last century, people shopped," Connor said.

"Huh?" I grunted.

"He's started one of his famous rants again," said Madi.

"Hear me out, guys. Before the internet was even thought of, stores were stacked with goods. There were clothes and many shops that sold them. There was music that had to be chosen, and books and accessories and all sorts of things that people bought. They went shopping."

"People can still shop on Social Media Central," said Madi. "People sell things all the time."

"But people had a sensory connection with what they chose to buy before they handed over their money. Plus, when they weren't shopping, people saw each other face to face by visiting each other's homes. So the books on their shelves, the records in their collections, the nicknacks they had around their homes, the clothes they wore, all of these things represented their identity when others came to visit."

"Connor, we get dressed up all the time."

"Because we're made to. We have to keep the glam factor while our fans hardly go out."

"When I was very young, my parents' car was some kind of status symbol," said Soho. He had been looking through the lens of one of the video cameras but joined our conversation instead. "People don't think of a car that way anymore. Hell, most of us don't even own one."

"Because we can share a picture of our dream car instead," Connor replied. "The internet took away the need to buy our identity and replaced it with a way to share our identity. Our generation has always shared the music we like, the images that appeal to us, and everything we think on a daily basis. We plug in and log on. If you look back at history, stores began to close when everyone went online."

"That's why I don't go near Social Media Central," I said.

"I still don't see your point," said Madi.

"Most of our identity lives online," the dancer clarified, after listening to us for a while. "But if you really think about it, Miss Madeline, you have friends you see all the time. You have Tayler, Connor, and that Shaun guy, who know the real you. Just the way my fellow dancers know what makes me happy, sad, or even horny for that matter. That's because we rehearse together all the time. But most people out there only connect on the ever-present SMC. I used to be one of them, thinking that my online identity *was* me, until I started dancing. Then I realized it was only the smallest part and my device was that prosthetic limb I wasn't even born with."

Soho applauded. I joined him. Connor shook the dancer's hand, and eventually, Madi nodded.

"We go live in seven minutes," called one of the camera operators.

"Everyone to your places," Soho commanded. "Go through your lines again, team. The autocue will help you."

The dancers scurried back behind the curtain, their feather boas waving behind them. The blond performer peeked out once more as we read our lines. Connor returned his gaze like a lover who was keeping their romance secret.

The minutes flew past, and before we knew it, Soho called, "Action!"

"All of us, everyone watching this stream, is lucky to live in Astra City," I said. "No, I'm serious. Just stop and think for a minute."

"The stores are always stocked with enough ingredients for any mirror meal you decide on." Connor sung this line. Soho grinned. "But take it from me, all those images I've shared of farmers growing that stuff—well, they were given to me to share."

Madi grabbed her prop sunglasses and shoved them on her face quicker than the snap of a mousetrap.

"The truth is, Astra City residents, your food is grown in a laboratory."

"But our education is first-rate," I continued. "New lessons are being developed daily for the school-aged and those needing to catch up."

Connor looked at me and asked, "Wouldn't kids prefer a live teacher to talk to? Once upon a time, you could research various websites. All different sites for people to read news, buy stuff, connect anonymously. You could create a website from scratch. But now there's only Social Media Central. The others were shut down a generation ago."

Soho covered his mouth, but he couldn't hide his laughter.

"Take it from me," Connor continued. "Social Media Central augments our reality, our version of it, at least. Keep that in mind the next time you talk to someone online. You'll have some wicked conversations!"

"So with just one central location," said Madi in overenthusiastic tones, "engage with your infinite world. No need for worries. No need for dramas. Just be the star of *your* life on Social Media Central."

The dancers darted in and around my friends while that blond guy shimmied up to me like a man trying to keep warm.

"And when will you be accessible on the all-knowing Social Media Central?" he asked.

"He's got a point, Tayler," said Connor. "How else will you tell people about Movie Night?"

"What's Movie Night?" the dancer asked.

Something possessed me. Probably the god of celebrity. That deity shot through my spine and into my jaw.

"We all have favorite movies, but we watch them alone."

"And why would we want to share the experience?" Connor prompted. He swayed with the dancers.

"So our friends and family understand us better." I still faced the blond, as if *he'd* asked the question.

"What a great idea," the dancer said.

He swirled around me and planted a kiss on my cheek. Madi jumped up so fast, the sunglasses flung off her face. She stormed past me, faced the camera, and announced, "The circus has arrived." Then she blew a kiss to our audience before strolling out of the camera's eye.

She never gave a reason for her actions when I questioned her later, and apologized for overreacting. She assured me it had nothing to do with that dancer's show of affection, and I had no reason to suspect it did. To my dismay, the reasons for her solo act would eventually become crystal clear.

# Nine

"I DON'T UNDERSTAND why you haven't moved out of your sad apartment," Connor said.

"I've been too busy running around with you lot."

He snapped a picture of some chic passerby. "Still, what if you invite a fan over, and they share photos of your place on the web?"

"That won't be happening any time soon. Madi and I are devoted to each other."

"Well, you were flirting with the male dancer the other day. And if I recall, you had your eye on Mike, that author from the book launch."

"Connor, not all of us are homosexual. Besides, that book launch was four weeks ago." I pulled out my new mobile screen and checked the date. "Actually, that was six weeks ago. Shit, time flies when you're having fun."

I grabbed a glass of champagne from the tray of a passing waiter. He strolled into the crowd of worshippers. Another day, another party. Their theme today was red, yet some astute designer painted all the walls black in this sumptuous space. Costumed bodies sparked like flames against the darkness.

Various members of our congregation stood around chatting, holding their screens tightly in one hand as if clutching a wad of cash. An overly tall woman with a metallic headdress stood as a beacon for these ships of the night. She was touched by wandering fingers desperate to feel every part of her outfit, crowning her the belle of the ball by their actions.

Her gaze fixed on mine, still displaying a tone of uber cool as she acknowledged who I was. And yet she never raised her small screen. A man in a blood-colored jacket stepped up to her and caressed the palm of her hand. Her head tilted. She half smiled. Then, he waltzed with her to an imaginary tune.

"There's something exotic in the air tonight," said Felicity. She had moseyed over with Shaun.

"Imagine our lives like theirs," he added. "Exotic and playful."

"Give it a rest, lover. I said I'd consider it."

"Consider what?" Connor asked.

"He wants me to be part of his blog in a new section called *Our Threesome Phase*."

"It's my way of including you in my daytime job," said Shaun.

"*Our Threesome Phase*?" I asked. "Are you serious?"

"Think about it, Tayler. Felicity wouldn't feel left out as I wander the earth making love."

"I knew what I was getting into before I started this relationship," she said. "Besides, my bookstore is expanding. Go off and have your fun. I'm not into other women." He smirked. "And don't even think of inviting another man into our bedroom." Shaun's jaw dropped.

"This sounds like a lover's quarrel," said Connor. "Tayler, you can play Agony Aunt. I've got the fabulous to photograph." He charged into the crowd, camera at the ready.

"Shaun, not everyone is into threesomes," I said. "Although most of this crowd seem like they're ready for an orgy. What's in this champagne?"

"It's spiked with a special blend."

"What?" Felicity and I examined our glasses. "Is it vodka?"

"No. It's a magic love potion of a chemical kind."

"I thought this champagne tasted extra sweet. Is it to hide the secret ingredient?"

"That can't be moral," said Felicity.

"It was the government's idea," Shaun replied. "But we warned the guests as they paid for their tickets online."

I studied the sediment at the bottom of my glass, then waved it in circles so the drugs could mix in.

"Most of this generation are still virgins," Felicity said. "They're entering uncharted territory tonight with no clue of what might eventuate. What on earth made them open up to experience?"

"It was Tayler talking about Movie Night," Shaun replied.

"I doubt that," I said. "I'd like to believe it was Movie Night and that somehow we made a difference, but I don't."

"Perhaps you did," said Felicity. "Don't underestimate yourself or the rest of your crew."

"Look at them. Somehow they've learned to talk to each other face to face. Some of them for the first time. And now they want to open up to real emotion. They want to find out about real love in all its forms."

"Be proud of what you achieved," said Shaun. We clinked glasses. "As the banner on my blog states, *the only way to really know a person is to make love to them*. And tonight, we're playing cupid."

"I'm still not convinced we did this. But whatever the reason, I think it's divine. Simply divine."

"Watch out, Tayler. Your chemicals are kicking in."

"I think it's the fall of the empire," said Felicity.

"My love, the empire has already fallen," Shaun said. "In an empty city of steel and glass, what textures are there for people to feel alive in? This is how we resurrect the empire."

"For a person who has sex with strangers, you can be awfully deep."

"It's because I only make love to the willing. That's how I stay connected to the human race."

They kissed. It was slow and sensual and mind-blowing to watch. I needed Madi, but she wasn't there that night. She said she wasn't feeling well, and that I should go with our friends. So I closed my eyes and imagined her lips on mine. It wasn't enough. I needed sex.

"I'm just going to the bathroom," said Shaun.

Felicity let go of him. He wandered past a row of our followers with their arms around each other's shoulders. They swayed, and yet in their state, no one stumbled off their feet. Soon they rubbed cheeks with the person to their right, then to their left. They kissed, again taking turns with the inebriated being on either side. The selection was random. Some girls kissed boys while boys kissed boys and girls kissed girls. It was wild!

"We're watching group sex unfold, Tayler."

"Real connection. I don't believe it."

"If Shaun's right, you've got a lot to be proud of with Movie Night. You've got people communicating again. Although, I didn't think it would lead to this."

"But it's not all chaos, Felicity. Can you imagine the conversations these people will have in the morning? We may be seeing the start of real friendship again. This has to be good. This is the end of loneliness."

"But what do adults with the communication skills of infants talk about after sex? There's a whole emotional level they've never experienced. Heartbreak, for instance. And jealousy. Let's not forget jealousy. This might rip them apart."

"Then let's hope they talk to other friends rather than taking solace in their mobile screens once more."

"They'll bully each other on Social Media Central. Like I said, this empire is going to fall."

The row of kissing individuals now broke off into twos. Their eagerness seemed violent, like they had a meal to devour that they had just hunted down.

"You stand aside from all of this, don't you?" she queried.

"Isn't that what you're doing?"

"You're very astute. My concern about you, Tayler, is that you may be flying too close to the sun."

"Huh?"

"I think you need to detach yourself more. At Mike's book launch, you were still the one who tagged along. Now you're one of them. A Social Media Socialite without a social media account."

"But Felicity, you want what I've got."

"Maybe. But I'm taking baby steps to get there. I'm older than you, more world-wise. You need to tread carefully before you realize you're in too deep."

Shaun returned. "I know a heavy conversation when I see one," he said.

His girlfriend and I nodded slowly.

"What were you talking about?"

She and I giggled.

"Tayler, what I like about you is that you can break all barriers, yet you don't even know it."

"He's right. You have that boy-next-door charm that everyone looks to for truth and genuine love," Felicity said. They cuddled.

I watched Connor in the distance.

"Don't look away. Accept a compliment with grace."

"I'm concerned about our friend," I said.

"Hear that?" said Shaun. "That's the sound of a sudden change in topic."

"Should we go along with it?"

"Let's."

"Okay, thanks for the compliment," I said.

They both grinned wholeheartedly.

"But one of the guests said something to me earlier," I added.

Now they rolled their eyes.

"No, listen. Do you know anything about Connor running for politics?"

"It's a phase he's going through," Shaun replied. "It's nothing serious."

"But the guy who asked me was dead serious."

"Who was he?"

I studied the crowd. "He's not here now, unless he's in the bathroom. Regardless, he was really questioning me about it. Asking me if Connor had any real plans to rally support."

"Maybe he wants to vote for him," said Felicity.

"It's a joke I ran on my blog," Shaun explained. "Even Connor changed his profile picture. He's in a robe with a weird gold-leaf thing on his head, like an ancient Roman senator or something."

"And what have our fans been commenting?" I asked.

"A few were actually encouraging. But I told them it was all a joke."

As if his ears were burning, Connor chose that moment to join us.

"Are the fabulous too drugged-out to photograph?" I asked.

"Not really," he replied. "I'm getting some of my best pictures. But I was desperate for conversation that actually made sense. What have I interrupted?"

"Strangely, we were talking about you," Felicity replied.

"About me? Whatever for?"

"Tayler was worried about some dude questioning your quest for power," Shaun replied.

The photographer scrunched his lips.

"Someone was asking if you were serious about going into politics. I told Tayler it was *our* joke," Shaun added.

Now our friend stared into space.

"Hmm. I know that face, Connor. *Are* you thinking about it?" Shaun asked.

"There's been talk."

"What talk?"

"A few fans have private-messaged me. They want me to seriously think about it."

"You don't want to do that, surely," said Felicity.

"I think you should," I said.

"I'd do a better job than the joker who pays us. And look at Movie Night. Our followers take note of what we put out there. How often do they listen to what we put out there for the government?"

"What would you rally for?" Felicity asked.

"More hobbies that bring people together. Cooking classes. Get people back into your bookstore to listen to authors read. Whatever works. Anything they used to do that made them socialize face to face."

"But wouldn't we lose our power as social media celebrities?" I asked.

He looked at me sternly. "Tayler, you of all people should understand where I'm coming from. There's real power in getting people to think for themselves. And I'll be the one to save them from boredom." He closed his eyes. "And I know that look, Shaun. You think I'm getting too big for my boots."

"Do you really want the responsibility that goes with all that when you can keep living the life of luxury on the payroll of the person you want to replace?"

"I think he *should* go into politics," said Felicity. "People need people. Not a watered-down version of them on Social Media Central."

"I think I need to pee," I said.

"You're looking spacey, Tayler," said Shaun. "Is your love drug kicking in?"

"Yep. I'm feeling strangely uplifted."

"Wait until you see the bathtub."

"Why?"

"You'll know when you get there."

I traced off. The chatter around me sounded like a recording played one octave too low. The mass of red paved the way to the toilet like a carpet rolled out for an old-fashioned first-night performance. Except this rug had holes. *Cigarette burns, perhaps?*

"Tayler, what movie do you think I should watch?"

"I don't know you from a bar of soap."

"Yes I know that, but what movie would make me understand you?"

"I really need to pee."

This stranger clutched the back of my neck and forced my lips to hers. Her tongue invaded. I pulled away.

"Go and pee," she said. "Let's continue this conversation when you get back."

I raised my finger for no particular reason and continued my journey. The brass knob creaked when I opened the door, and as I entered, I nearly fell into a glossy black bathtub. One end was raised for proper back support while its base sprouted claws like a creature from myth. My distorted reflection peered back from its base.

*Classy.*

I never knew if wood was the right material for a toilet seat. I understood the bathroom had a classic theme, but I had to ponder if organic materials were as hygienic as a good solid plastic seat. In this case, black would have suited the color scheme. The timber grain just looked old and cheap.

My urine smelled as if it could burn mold off grubby tiles just with its vapors. It could blind small animals. It could cure a runny nose. I flushed.

The period sink with its chunky curved corners and metallic crosses on each of its taps for ease of turning, was the next thing to greet me in my ritual of relief. And the clunky ceramic was darker than dark.

"Back to black," I said to myself.

This was more like it. This went with the bathtub, not with the toilet. I picked up the amber-colored soap and took in its floral, forest, milky—*what does it smell like?* I sniffed my lathered fingers. *A hint of pear, detergent, and a lingering citrus note. Yep, that's it.*

Someone walked in, snapping me out of whatever trance I was in. My reflection looked back at me sheepishly. I strode back into the party.

"Tayler!" It was that girl again—the one who'd tried to rape my tonsils. "Who are you looking for?"

"My friends."

"You mean Shaun and Felicity? They left. Connor is just over there if you want him."

Connor was busy talking to one of the guests.

"I don't think I should bother him."

"So what movie should I watch if I want to get into your head?"

"I don't know. *Beyond the Valley of the Dolls*, perhaps. *They're a Weird Mob.*" I scanned the room as I mentioned the last title.

"Does Madeline Q let you out to play?"

"Not really."

"But she's at home not feeling well."

"How did you know that?"

She displayed her small screen.

"Stupid me. She posted it."

"Tayler, I'm your biggest fan."

I laughed. "That's not a very original line. Who are you anyway?"

"Oops." She looked at the ceiling before digging her hand into the pocket of the retro airline costume she was wearing. She pulled out a name tag and pinned it on. "That's me."

"Grace," I read. "Hmm. So, Grace, why are you my biggest fan?"

"Because you're dreamy. Your boyish looks wet my pants."

"Yuck! Felicity was right."

"What do you mean?"

"You're all too childish to understand seduction."

"Shaun wouldn't agree with you."

"How would you know what Shaun thinks?"

"I read his blog."

"Really? Well, I know him personally, and trust me, face-to-face contact whether in conversation or through lovemaking, is the way to get to know a person. Shit. It's his motto. The only way to know a person is to, you know, fuck them."

She undid her top button. I flung my arm out toward her like an out-of-control crane on a building site. I think this odd move was my attempt to stop her. I pulled in my wayward limb and turned to step forward. As the crowd gyrated in their own fertility dance, metallic robots charged through the front door. I rubbed my eyes before taking another glass of champagne from the tray of a startled waitress. My vision cleared.

The cyborgs were actually police in helmets with bulletproof glass and shiny metal breastplates featuring built-in face-recognition software. And they carried compact stun guns that reminded me of a toy laser I had as a kid.

Photos again. Our congregation had not lost touch with their mobile screens after all. They were snapping away with the frenetic energy of a tribe of percussionists.

"You're Tayler," called one of the cops from a distance. In no time, he was by my side.

"Yes, I am."

"Okay, everyone," shouted another. "Party's over. I need you all to leave."

"What's going on?" I asked.

"Do you know this woman?" He showed me a picture of a young Asian girl with long blue hair.

"What a great image. What model screen is that? The colors are so vibrant."

"Don't be a smart-ass. Do you know this woman?"

"No."

"Are you sure? Look again."

"Officer, blue hair on an Asian chick is something I wouldn't forget in a hurry."

At this stage, the officers were pushing the dazed crowd out the door. Connor caught my eye and shrugged as he was moved outside.

"What's all this about? Who is that girl?"

"That's what we're trying to find out."

"Why?"

"She was found dead in the bathtub a moment ago."

# Ten

"MADI, YOU CAME to support me," I said. "You shouldn't have. You're not well."

"No, I'm here at the police station because I was told to come in."

Connor moved down a seat so she could sit next to me.

"What happened?" she asked.

"Apparently someone died," Connor said.

"I know that, but who was she?"

"Someone with blue hair who none of us remembers," Shaun replied.

"Blue hair? You'd have to remember that." She sniffled. "Connor, do you have a spare hanky?"

He passed one to her. She blew her nose before clutching the handkerchief to her chest. I gazed out a window that had not seen a cleaning rag for at least three months. Small globes lit the brittle yellow lawn outside, which looked sharp enough to scratch the ankles of those who dared cut it. Overgrown bushes fought for space toward the front fence. And one single tree sprouted purple flowers, claiming it alone was the star of the garden.

"I'm still high from whatever was in that champagne," I confessed. I turned to Shaun. "Where's Felicity?"

"They didn't contact her, so I left her at home," he replied.

"They're going to want to see her once they know she was there." I studied my friends to see if they agreed.

"Should I say she was there?"

"They're going to work it out once they view the online pictures."

"But not many people were taking photos," Shaun reasoned. "Hardly anyone was, really. They were discovering my favorite pastime."

"It's best to tell the truth," said Connor.

"Yes, it is," sniffed Madi.

We all stared out the window.

"Okay, that girl..." Connor gazed into space. "I've gone through my photos, and as far as I can tell, she wasn't at the party."

"So how was she found in the bathtub?" I asked. "I mean, Connor, you have the only accurate record of this evening's party. Like Shaun said, everyone was too busy trying to get it on to share anything on Social Media Central. Well, at least until the cops showed up."

Madi sprung up as if her flu had magically vanished. "Imagine the images that would've ended up online if our followers had sex."

"Trust you to think of that," Connor replied. "By the way, I've already posted my photos to SMC. They might help clear this mess up."

Four police officers strode in our direction like classroom bullies. They weren't wearing their helmets, but their breastplates each shot a fluctuating beam in our direction. One cop pointed at me and called my name before telling me to follow him. As I stood, my friends were also commanded to follow each of the other officers separately.

Inside the interview room, a woman out of uniform asked me to sit down and then left me alone for ten minutes. I pulled out my small screen and flicked through Connor's images of the party. Dozens of people flashed by, but no one with unnatural hair color.

"Nice of you to join us." The woman had returned with a larger screen. She sat opposite me and put her device on the table between us. "Now, you may not realize this, Tayler, but I'm a fan of yours."

"Really? You?"

"Why do you find that hard to believe?"

"Excuse me, I didn't mean to be rude. Sometimes, I get taken aback by the people who take an interest in me."

"Out of all your friends, you're the most like me. You're the shy one without a voice."

"Um, I used to be."

"Tell me, the idea of Movie Night, that was yours, wasn't it?"

"It was half mine. A guy called Mike—"

"That author from a couple of months back."

"Yep, that's the one. I'm surprised you remember him."

"I told you, I'm one of your fans. I always search for news on you."

"Well, he came up with the idea of sharing a book with a loved one. I pointed out that no one reads anymore and that people should share movies."

"I finally know my father, thanks to you and Mike."

"Really?"

"We're going to a restaurant tonight and will be actually sitting face to face for the first time in three years."

"That's an expensive night for a police officer." I covered my mouth. "Sorry, I didn't mean to be rude again."

"Oh, that's okay. We've been saving up for a while now. My dad said restaurants and cafés were a dime a dozen in his youth."

"And now they're only for the elite."

"I bet you and your friends eat out all the time."

"Actually, we don't. We eat in a lot, and Shaun finally convinced me to mirror meal, but none of us are from a generation who ever thought of eating out. Do you mind if I ask what movie brought you and your dad together?"

"He wanted me to watch *Holly Dances Alone*."

"I like that film. It's one of the few recent ones that makes sense."

"It made me understand how he felt when my mother left."

"He raised you?"

She nodded. "And he always seemed angry when I was growing up." She gazed over my shoulder, looking as lost as a child whose pet had just run off. "Silly me, talking about my private life."

"Sorry I'm late." A bulky officer charged in, took off his helmet, and scanned me with his breastplate. "So, you're Tayler. One of social media's best. Well, that reputation means nothing to me."

I leaned forward and sat my elbows on the table. "I'm not in the mood for the good-cop, bad-cop routine."

"Now you listen here—"

I raised the palm of my hand. "Seriously, my taxes don't pay your wages so you can abuse me. I'm the public you're supposed to be protecting. Now if you can't speak in a civil tone, then I'd prefer you to leave."

The woman placed her hand on the power-obsessed officer's shoulder. "Let me handle this," she told him. "Tayler, tell us what you know about the girl who died. Did you talk to her?"

"I don't remember even seeing her. But then, it was a drug-fueled party. Perhaps she came later and I didn't notice her. It does sound strange, though. I had just taken a pee and saw the bathtub. If anyone had killed anyone in that tub, they did it in record speed."

"Were you on anything that may have altered your perception of time?"

"Maybe."

"Which drug did you take?"

"I'm not sure, but it made a lot of people horny."

"Ah, it's that new love-potion thing they're selling," the male officer said.

"See, you can be nice." He huffed. "How long has it been on the market?"

"I think that one's been around for about a month," the woman replied.

"It's been upgraded," her fellow officer said. "I tried it last week. Trust me, it's a better recipe."

"I didn't get to make love on it. I was hauled here for questioning."

The male wagged his finger. "Make sure you have sex when you get home."

"Now, Tayler, back to the woman." She displayed the dead girl's picture on her screen. The victim wore a cheeky grin and had fake pussycat ears clipped to her signature blue hair. "Think hard. She was there. You must have seen her."

I looked closer. I shook my head. "Seriously, she's too unique not to remember."

The officer waved her hand above the screen to display the next picture. I shivered. She slept like an angel in that same black bathtub. I picked up the device and studied the image carefully, startled at how peaceful this dead girl looked and how perfectly framed the image was.

"Tell us about your night," the male cop said.

I shut my eyes and drew a breath. I went through every detail I could recall. My small talk with friends. My advice to Felicity, which they wanted me to elaborate on. Connor's proposed rise in politics. The first sense of the chemical take over. That clueless girl who clutched onto my mouth like a bear trap.

"It must be great to be you," the female officer said.

"My luck changed when I met Madeline Q."

"Where was she?" the male asked. "You two are like conjoined twins."

"She's not well."

"She's well enough to come down to the station."

I giggled.

"What's so funny?"

"It's nothing. Forget it."

"Tell us. Did you remember something?"

"No. It's just that phrase. *Come down to the station.* People will go *up* to shake your hand. They'll travel *up* to the coast. But they never come *up* to the station. Why is that?"

The female turned to her partner. "Is this an effect of the drug?"

He nodded.

"Sorry. We were talking about Madi. She's sniffling her nose off at the moment."

"Strange that she wasn't at a party where a girl lost her life," stated the male cop. He crossed his arms.

"Why is that strange?"

"Well, like I said before, you two are like conjoined twins, and it just seems odd she avoided a party where a murder occurred."

"No, there's nothing odd about it."

"Come on, Tayler. That girlfriend of yours had a *convenient* excuse not to attend that particular event."

"Really? I'd call a cold an *inconvenient* reason not to attend."

"Don't be stupid. She wouldn't miss the opening of an email, let alone an extravaganza centered on the color of her hair!" He looked at me quizzically. "You have heard of that old-fashioned thing they used to call an email?"

I leaned back in my chair. "What do they say about assumptions, Officer?"

The female cop smirked.

"When you assume, you make an *ass* out of *you* and *me*. Well, in this case, just you."

He jumped out of his chair.

"Now, it is true that Madeline will attend any party anywhere. She just has to have a whiff of alcohol, and she follows the scent like a hawk zeroing in on prey. But that's what she's paid to do. In fact, it's what we're all paid to do. It's our job."

"Hold on," said the female. "You're paid to be at these parties?"

I felt my teeth bite my lower lip. "Isn't it the dead girl we're supposed to be talking about?"

They shared a sly glance. "Okay, you're free to go. But don't leave town."

"Why would I? I'm keen to get to the bottom of this."


"MY LAWYER WAS as sharp as a tack," said Connor. "What's the matter? Didn't you ask for a lawyer? Oh, Tayler!"

"It didn't cross my mind."

"What did you say?"

"Only what I knew."

Shaun pressed the button on the blender, creating his own original cocktail. We had been taking turns using whatever was in Connor's fridge to come up with these concoctions. Shaun poured his latest creation into our long-stemmed glasses. I sniffed the white sludge. It had a lychee smell, but I hadn't seen any fruit going into the recipe. I sipped. All I tasted was gin.

"Should you be drinking?" I asked Madi.

"Lover, this is our first run-in with the law. And it's over a guest at one of our parties. Cold or no cold, I'm settling my nerves."

"So who do you think she was?" Shaun wondered. "We all saw her picture."

"She didn't seem dead," I said. They looked at me as if I'd just farted. "No, seriously. I have never seen a dead person, but she didn't look like someone who'd gone through trauma. She just looked like she was taking a nap."

"Don't all dead people look like they're sleeping?"

"I don't know, Shaun, but something doesn't feel right about this." I sipped, ignoring the tart taste of liquor in my drink.

"Did you see the snapshot of her in the furry cat ears?" Connor asked.

We all nodded.

"She doesn't look like one of our regulars. She's the right age bracket, but there's something independent about her," Connor commented.

"You're interpreting a lot based on a picture," said Madi.

"I take photos of our followers every day. I know what they look like. They have that same doe-eyed expression with each image. Except for tonight, though. A light bulb has gone on behind their vacant eyes. Well, at least for most of them."

"I'd say the light went on in their hearts," Shaun added.

"What? Heartburn?"

"They're starting to feel. Maybe even think. It's a shame they didn't get to make love."

"Back to our girl," I said. "She's unique. She's definitely no clone. She's flirty. She's cheeky, which means she has brains."

"Flirty means she has brains?" Madi queried.

"Well, look at you. You're sexy and you knew how to flirt with me from the start. That takes brains."

"Or heart," said Shaun.

"But coming from the heart means you have intuition. Intuition is a marriage between heart and mind. Dumb people don't get that."

"You're being mighty cosmic, Tayler," Connor alleged. "Are the chemicals still in your system?"

I tried my best look of innocence.

"But he's right," said Shaun. "I'm careful about who I sleep with. If I don't sense emotional intelligence I steer clear."

"I also like her sense of style," Madi added. "Blue hair. Who does that these days? She's an original."

"A toast to an original," I cried. We clinked glasses. "Has anyone checked Social Media Central?"

"Good point," said Shaun. "Everyone will be talking about who this woman was."

"What the...?" Madi glared at her screen as if her fans had turned on her.

"What's the matter?"

She rotated her device so that we all saw her home page. In bold letters at the top were the words 'Vale Petra.' Underneath was the same photo of the dead girl in fake cat ears the policewoman had shown me. And under her image was a commentary about her fashion sense.

My girlfriend shook her head. "Who's hacked into my account?" The others checked their profiles.

"Mine's okay," said Shaun.

"Have you tried to log in?" Connor asked. "Mine won't accept my password."

"Oh my!" Madi squealed. She read from her screen. "Petra was a woman who time forgot. Colored hair that made her a throwback to a long-lost generation, and ridiculous accessories more suited to a child's doll." Madi became teary. "Cat ears, for example. Her friends reported these were regular attachments. What was she trying to prove?" She tossed the diseased gadget on the kitchen counter. "I can't read anymore. It's so bitchy."

"Honey, you were born bitchy," said Connor.

"Not online. Well, not in the articles I write on fashion, and definitely not when talking about the dead."

"Guys, I can't log in," Shaun cried.

My friends stared at each other as if death was waiting to take them all. I wandered to the food processor and created the strongest cocktail I could.

# Eleven

SOMETHING STOPPED ME in my tracks. Like a parent eavesdropping on their teenage daughter, I stood at my landlady's door.

"You know, you're my closest friend," she said to whichever acquaintance happened to be appearing on her screen today. "You don't know how hard it is for a woman my age to find friends."

I zoned out after that line. My mind ticked over. I knew about her country childhood where her parents were proactive in the neighborhood. They'd encourage the kids on their street to play together, while they entertained the other adults with delectable banquets. Both generations handed over their screens before entering their house. Mary would share tales of the kid's games they used to play, a series of tasks requiring imagination.

By the time she was twenty-one, her heart had been broken. A city lad with too much money and charisma told her everything a young woman expects to hear. For several years, they'd planned to travel around the country or board a jet for Spain. But he set out on the adventure by himself, shooting her a message when he was far out of reach.

Then there was the other love she rarely talked about. I learned not to ask.

But she did talk to me about many things. Food was a favorite topic. She'd often repeat the words of her mother saying how important it was to know how to cook meals to keep a man, and sugary treats to keep the young ones smiling. And sometimes when she knocked at my door with yet another dinner invitation, I'd wonder if she'd have a mystery guest.

Over time, I met Claudia, a childhood friend who'd visit from afar, and Simone and Desmond, work colleagues who liked to gossip.

A while ago, Mary and her workmates had been ordered to log in from home, never needing to venture through their office doors again. I'd still see Claudia or Simone and Desmond when they knocked on my door looking for Mary. We'd hear her chatting with whomever, but as we called her name, no more words would be uttered.

I comforted her forgotten friends several times, through tears, anger, and regret. And they comforted me through the same feelings of loss I didn't expect to have.

And now my habit of silently listening to the buddy I lost happened every time I needed to visit. Like a father desperate to get close to his child, I'd try to get a glimpse of her world. When I felt ready to dispense with my despair, I'd force a grin and reach for the doorknob.

"I've run out of cat food, Mary," I said. "Do you have any?"

"You don't have any cats."

"Yes I do. Yours have been living at my place for weeks now."

My landlady studied her lounge room.

"You didn't even realize they were gone, did you?"

"Why did you take them?"

"Because you weren't feeding them."

"Is that Tayler?" came a voice from her computer screen. It was her romantic interest.

"Hi, Bernard."

"Hi, Tayler. What do you know about the murder?"

"What murder?"

"There was a dead girl in the bathtub," Mary replied. "It's all we Amazing Seven ever talk about."

"Yes, there was a dead girl, so we've been told, but no one's said anything about murder. Hold on, when did the Amazing Twenty become the Amazing Seven?"

"When Caroline started bitching about me behind my back. Bernard told me all about it, didn't you, Bernard?"

"Yep. She was private-messaging me all sorts of nasty things about Mary. To cut a long story short, our tribe split. The lion's share took Caroline's side."

"So what do the others call themselves? The Breakaway Thirteen?"

"Anyway, you shouldn't be hanging around with that social media set," said Mary. "Did you read what Madeline Q said about that poor Petra?"

"She didn't write that. Her account was hacked."

"Still, I don't like you running with that lot."

"Mary, you thought she was royalty the first time I mentioned her."

"I can leave you two to talk privately if you want," said Bernard.

"It's okay," I said. "It's not really a private conversation."

"Mary does have a point, Tayler. Madeline Q and her offsider, Connor, throw those parties."

"And that nice Shaun does as well," Mary added. "But he's too nice to be involved in the murder."

"For goodness sake," I screeched. "We just have a dead body! And if there was a murderer, it could have been anyone at the party."

"So why are Madeline and Connor suspects?"

"There has to be proof of a murder before there are suspects. And the weird thing is, none of us remember that girl at the party."

"All the same, I'm happy to leave you two to talk," said Bernard.

"There's no need to disconnect."

"It's okay, darling," said my landlady. "You can go." She glared at me as if she was constipated.

I shrugged, confused by her mood. "Bye, Bernard."

"Bye, my love. Bye, Tayler."

I waved goodbye at the screen. His video image disappeared.

"How come I never see you anymore, Tayler?"

"Because you never answer your door."

"That never stopped you from barging in before."

"Well, I'm busy now. I have a life." I gestured at her computer. Next to it was a pile of unopened envelopes containing rent money. I had left them under her front door in the past weeks. "You haven't been to the bank for a while. I can set up a regular online cash transfer if you prefer."

"No, Tayler. We talked about this when you moved in. Cash only. I don't want the tax man knowing my affairs."

"Mary, most of your private information is online, including your bank details." The jingle of a melodic wind chime came from her screen. "What's that?"

"That will be Cassidy." She lowered her voice. "He's a married man." She winked.

"You sly old devil. What will the Amazing Seven think about your two-timing?"

"He's one of the Amazing Seven." She smirked like a teen boy who'd just discovered masturbation.

"Mary, are you there?" asked a voice. He sounded younger than my gray-haired landlady, but his tone was as smooth as an old-world crooner.

"Answer," Mary commanded. Instantly, his image appeared. I looked twice. I imagined Cassidy on some thrilling adventure to the Amazon, encountering pigmy cannibals and fighting his way out of danger with his bare fists. *What on earth can this handsomely rugged guy see in musty old Mary?*

"You're Tayler, aren't you?"

"Yes," she replied on my behalf. "This is my lodger, the famous Tayler."

"You must be going through hell, you poor man. Are you a suspect in the murder?"

"For the last time, there is no murder."

"What are you talking about? Everyone is gossiping about it on Social Media Central."

Cassidy disappeared as various blogger front pages flashed up on the screen. All of them carried Petra's trademark pussy-eared picture. One got straight to the point with the simple headline—*Murder!*

"Is the whole world going mad? Yesterday, we were at the police station being questioned about her. None of us remembered seeing her at all. And at no stage did the cops implicate us in her supposed murder."

Another page appeared on the screen. It was the blog of the Astra Detective Squad. The policewoman who interviewed me the day before was featured on a small profile pic in the top corner. I drifted toward the computer. She had written a piece about our mystery girl's murder and how Madeline Q and Connor were suspects.

"See, I told you not to run with that crowd," said Mary.

Cassidy's face reappeared on the screen. "It sounds like the force might know something today that they didn't know yesterday."

My hands flew into the air of their own accord. "What's got into this crazy city? Seriously, all we've seen is a photo of that girl with her eyes shut in the same bathtub that was at the place where the party was. And Madi wasn't even at the party. She had a cold. And even if she was, she's not a cold-hearted killer. None of them are. Connor isn't. And Shaun, he's definitely not. I mean, what motive would they have to kill a fabulous nobody?"

"Well, the police seem to think they've got a case," Cassidy said. "And why did you bring Shaun into the conversation? He hasn't been implicated. Hmm, curious."

"What about all the other guests that were there? They haven't been questioned. Hold on a second. Can you bring the detective home page back up?"

Mary's guest obliged.

I read carefully. "You know what? Madi's account got hacked, and the others couldn't sign in. Perhaps this is a false post. Maybe they've been hacked as well? What if someone's out to get us?"

Lover-boy's image reappeared. "Sorry, Tayler. I know I hardly know you. Hell, I've just met you. But you're sounding a touch deluded."

"He's right," Mary alleged. "They're not your friends, Tayler. Just stay home for a while until this thing blows over."

"You're not listening, either of you." My hand slapped my forehead as if a mosquito had landed on it. "One, Connor was taking photos the whole time before the cops burst in. Two, Madi wasn't even at the party. Three, none of the Social Media Socialites have a motive. And four, how come none of the other guests are suspects? One of them could have met her and for some outlandish reason, killed her. Hell, and what if this Petra woman simply had a drug overdose? We were all high at the party."

"You need to rest, Tayler," Mary advised. "If the detectives say there's been a murder, then there's been a murder. Just be thankful you're not a suspect."

I screamed. Instantly my mobile device rung, saving my throat from getting raw by ending my howl for sanity. Madi's crying face appeared on the screen.

# Twelve

"OUR SOCIAL CALENDAR has dried up," Madi said. Her voice quivered like custard.

I walked through her front door. "Darling, apparently you're a suspect in that girl's murder."

"What!"

"You didn't know?" I pulled out my own gadget and showed her the detective department blog. "Makes your social calendar seem irrelevant, doesn't it?"

She slumped slightly, and I grabbed onto her elbows to support her. We staggered to her bedroom. Her face resembled a baby bird too scared to take its first flight. I carefully lowered her onto her designer houndstooth bedcover.

I hurried to the kitchen, opened her fridge, and found a half-empty bottle of vodka. I mixed it with orange juice in two tall glasses and carried both back to Madi.

We sipped for a long time in what seemed a sadder room, both seated on her bed. The two framed video screens that hung on her feature wall shed no light. These messengers of evil had been powered down, keeping their chaos well away from my tired princess.

She stared at the wall, a faded star burned by the wannabes that made her. That fickle bunch who found things worth posting on Social Media Central thanks to Madi, had now popped her away in a folder marked "curious misfits."

And it shamed me that for a dark moment I wondered where my star was now that hers had fallen. I gulped a mouthful of my drink.

"Do you want to stay with me?"

"I'm here, aren't I?"

"But you should distance yourself from me so you don't lose your celebrity status. Start your own blog or something."

"What if it gets hacked?"

She shrugged. "What I'm trying to say is I release you, if that's what you want."

"Ms. Madeline Q, I'm not going anywhere. Being with you has nothing to do with a horde of followers or a rise in social standing. I'm here because of the heart that beats behind that seductive veil of red hair. I'm here because of the sharp mind that ticks like a clock behind those mysterious eyes. Do I need to go on?"

"You're too good for me. If you really knew me, you'd run."

I sat up and leaned over to kiss her. "What don't I know?"

"Why I came to Astra City." She looked worried. "You see, Tayler, I came here when I was twenty-three."

"I know."

"I left a bad relationship."

"Go on."

"It was my second bad relationship." She gripped her vodka glass. "My first boyfriend was okay, I thought. I believed he loved me. We'd talk constantly about our imaginary wedding, and each time we spoke, we had a new scenario. We talked about it so often the scenarios became ludicrous. We dreamed up our underwear wedding, our Tupperware party wedding, and some silly wedding where we'd substitute ourselves for dogs and not tell the guests."

Her old smile returned. "That's the one we carried on about for hours."

"What went wrong?"

"I was nineteen and foolish." She took a measured sip. "I fell pregnant."

"Go on."

"That's when he broke up with me."

"Where's the child now?"

"There's no child, Tayler. I had an abortion."

"Go on."

"You're not judging me?"

"Madi, life in the mid-twenty-first century is complicated. Why would I judge you?"

"I dunno."

"You said you left a second bad relationship to come to Astra City."

"I had to escape in the dead of night from that one. I was a scrawny frightened girl too scared to say the wrong thing. If I did"—she raised her fist—"then wallop! I had too many beatings to understand my true worth." She paused.

"You don't need to continue."

She exhaled. "So Tayler, Madeline Q is a sham. She's a fake identity to run from my past."

"So what is your name?"

"Oh, my name is Madi, I just invented the persona to go with it."

"Have either of your exes been in touch with you?"

"The first one, no. The second one died in a fight." She chuckled. "Sweet justice, isn't it?"

"I guess it is." I laughed too. "I still don't see any reason to run from you, Madi."

She caressed my chin. "I don't deserve you, Tayler. You should find a woman who's real. One that doesn't live for the limelight."

I kissed her tenderly. Her vodka-flavored lips slipped over mine. This was my safe place, and I prayed it was still hers. I tried to breathe in her doubt, hoping to uncover the girl she once was before Astra City helped her hide.

"Damn it!" My screen was chiming.

"Ignore it," she said. She brushed her hair aside. "Who is it? No, ignore it. No, who is it? Don't look at me like that. You know I'm addicted."

"It's Connor." We both stared at the gadget.

"Answer it."

"Hello. What? No!"

THE POLICE WERE turning his place upside down, and they had a lot of ground to cover.

"Ms. Q, your place is next," said one of them. His breastplate shot a laser, which scanned us from head to toe. "Yes, Tayler is identified." He spoke into his screen.

Another cop was taking the portraits off the wall. "Be careful with that one," yelled Connor.

"What exactly are you looking for?" I asked.

Not one of them answered.

"You are trespassing and searching for god knows what. A knife? A gun? A melon-baller?"

Still no reply.

"Oh I forgot. It's an imaginary murder. I think the imaginary murder implements are hidden in the bottom kitchen drawer."

A pudgy one proceeded to the kitchen.

Connor paced, at times heading for a particular officer as if he was going to stop them. When one of them examined a collection of vintage cameras on a bureau, Connor marched up and watched from behind. But then another played with the intricate glass figurines on a display shelf, making Connor charge him, then stop out of caution.

On a table next to me was a cardboard box with no lid to hide what was kept inside. I stepped closer.

"Oh my," I murmured.

"What?" Madeline asked.

"I've only seen these in old movies."

"In old movies? Tayler, there's several of them being taken off the walls."

"But they're *professional* photos. These are snapshots."

"Hold on," called one of the cops. He turned to an associate. "Have we finished with the pictures in that box?" His workmate shrugged. "Okay, just flick through them, but don't take them out of the apartment."

I was already running my fingers over one with a glossy sepia surface. It showed a man and a woman in suits and the shiniest shoes I'd ever seen. Their hats were cylindrical with tassels attached to their tops, totally out of character with their glam appearance. Patterns reigned in the frame, from the sofas they sat in to the rug on the floor, all in monochromatic glory.

The next was in faded color and presented a younger version of Connor, his auburn eyes shining through studious glasses. I picked it up and was about to show Madi, until I realized it couldn't be him. I mean, only professional photos were printed in this day and age. Snapshots were taken, uploaded and forgotten.

This ancestor looked at me, calming me with his faraway gaze and self-assured smile. A natural face not contorted for an egocentric selfie. A man content in his time and place.

"Where are you, Tayler?" Madeline asked.

"Lost in the past."

She strolled to the fridge and took out a bottle of gin. The policeman searching the drawers looked her up and down, like an alley cat eyeing the sophisticated feline that's out of his league. She pulled out her keys and dropped them on the bench.

"Here. If you're doing my place next, you might as well search the joint without me there. Pop the keys in my mailbox when you're done. 237 Crescent Lane, but I'm sure you already know that. You still have a spare set, don't you, Tayler?"

I nodded.

"Great. You're good to go." She added the gin to four glasses already half filled with ice, leaving one for the officer. "Appreciation for your hard work."

She handed one to Connor who was now studying the man going through his underwear drawer. Madi jerked her head toward the front door. She led, he followed. As they passed me, I received my drink, and we all went outside to sit on the wooden stairs.

"Admit it, Connor," she said. "That one going through your undies is hot."

"Oh yes," he replied. "I wanted to help him try on some of the supposed evidence."

"I still don't see how they can do this," I said. "Show me a dead body, and I'll show you a potential murder. Or a death through explainable circumstances."

"So what is this really about?" Connor searched his ice cubes for an answer.

"Well, all I know is it takes one dead girl to kill our social calendar," Madi replied.

"Does that mean we're off the government payroll?" I asked.

She raised a brow. "I never thought of that."

"That's the least of our troubles," Connor said. "Have you been reading the news?"

"Not today. My stupid screens haven't been on since last night," Madi answered.

"And I've only looked at mine when someone's pointed out something I should look at," I said.

"Well, Madeline and Tayler, guess what? The world has officially gone mad. The trial starts next week."

"With what evidence?"

"None it seems. Just the image of a girl in a tub. But the online vote goes live on Monday. We'll be guilty or not guilty with the collective click of mouses."

My friends stared into space.

"Connor, have you been taking your running in politics thing a bit more seriously?" I asked.

"Kind of. The police who were questioning me brought it up."

"That's strange."

"Not really. It was on Shaun's blog."

"And you don't see a connection between all that has happened, and an online joke about you wanting power?"

"Online, it was a joke. In private messages, I was more serious. My real thoughts weren't in the public domain."

"Social Media Central is not a healthy place for us at the moment." Madi held up her device. Its screen was blank. "Seriously, team, turn them off."

"But you need to keep one step ahead of what's going on," I said.

"But every time I see my own blog, there's a new post about my supposed jealousy of Petra. That's why my screens are off."

"What?" I asked. "Why didn't you say something?"

"I was going to until you strolled through my door to tell me I was a suspect for murder. After that, it just didn't seem relevant."

"What did the blog say?"

"There were other pictures of Petra, like glamour shots. And whoever is pretending to be me said these were the fashion crimes of a desperate kid, or something to that effect."

"You seem lighthearted about it."

"I'm a tough girl, Tayler. You know that."

I grinned before turning to Connor. "What has your lawyer said?"

"None of them are returning my calls. It's so strange. Even the ones that have blogged in our favor have had their profiles removed."

Madi rested her forehead in the palm of her hand. "Fuck." I placed my arm around her shoulders. "And I just gave that moron my keys."

"Darling," I said. "What are they going to find? The poison lipstick you loaned Petra when you chatted in the bathroom of the party you never attended?"

"Yeah, I know you're right, dear, but it doesn't stop me worrying. I feel like I haven't slept in days. Oh wait! I haven't slept in days."

"Me neither," Connor added. "Have you read what they've been saying about us on Social Media Central?"

We both looked at him.

"Oh, I forgot. You've been hiding from the drama. Apparently, I'm a devious voyeur taking shots of only the beautiful people. Or I'm a spotlight avoider, hiding behind the lens."

"A spotlight avoider?" I queried. "That's so lame."

"I'm the mystery man weaving like gas around the real stars."

"Real stars!" shrieked Madi. "Do those little upstarts know who the real stars are?"

"Hello, does Connor live here?"

We stood, peering down toward the female voice who asked that question. With her signature blue hair, Petra smiled as she made her way up the stairs. Her eyes sparkled like a girl with a crush.

I turned to my companions. "Well, at least now we can identify the body."

# Thirteen

THE GIRL FORMERLY known as Petra stood by my side. Two days had passed since she popped into our lives from nowhere. The odd thing was, her real name was Candy. Seriously, it was! She was never a Petra, which made this whole thing an even bigger mind-fuck.

"So this is justice," I said. I gazed into the crowd.

"I'm glad I helped." She fondled her blue hair which covered the tassels of her flapper dress. It was a darker shade than her hairstyle, navy with intricate cobalt stitching. I'd helped her pick it out.

"When do you go back home?" I asked.

"In two days."

"Oh, that's right. I forgot." Again, I watched the crowd.

"Your mind is still preoccupied, Tayler. It has been the entire time I've been in town."

Candy was right, of course. Madi and Connor's now pointless court case was no longer online. It had vanished as if it never was. That same horde of followers who'd turned against them the previous week were now throwing a party in their honor. Correction, *our* honor. I had finally read some of the posts about me.

The week before, I was a "designer fuck." Now, Madi and I were the perfect couple. A few days past, I was the wannabe who should just go find his own online life. Now, I had a life. Before, I was guilty by association. That night, I was an honored guest at the 1920s Dames and Gangsters bash thrown by our followers.

There was one condition, though. Madeline Q, Connor, and Shaun had to choose a fabulous nobody—our words, not theirs—to accompany them. I got out of the deal by choosing Candy. Somehow, that was acceptable to our public.

"What's thrown you most about this past week?" Candy asked.

"Everything."

"Everything?"

"Everything. From how fickle this mob are to how heavy-handed the law came down on us for no reason." I took in her flirty grin. "And yet everything has been forgotten. Well, almost." I bit my lip before I mentioned that the government had stopped employing us. Fortunately, I'd been living off my healthy bank balance. "And here you are, a girl who recently posed for a few arty shots, and one of them was used to frame my friends. So, with no actual dead body, my friends were guilty until proven innocent."

She studied me. "I don't believe that's the only thing on your mind."

"These people in front of us are letting us keep the door takings, yet last week we were social media poison. And here you are—the dead girl. Yet you were never dead."

"Tayler, you're a broken record. You've been saying the same thing since I met you. But something else is on your mind. I'm sure of it."

Madi stood in pale gray fabric that trailed on the carpet. However, next to her stood a woman whose overly pink dress hugged her like a straitjacket. At times, her laugh could frighten small forest creatures. And many guests had made the mistake of thinking she had a bun in the oven as she snatched the canapés carried by waiters who tried to dash past.

Connor's date seemed to be the pick of the crop until he opened his mouth. He wore rounded glasses like mine, although his were infinitely cooler. In different lights, they changed color. Hues of dark red became chocolate or charcoal as he weaved through the crowd with his chosen celebrity. But tonight, Connor didn't carry a camera. He had no need. He couldn't log in to upload, anyway.

But back to his date. Tall and dreamy, with a voice that could curdle milk. His conversation was only about his mother or his father. Both were on their fourth marriage and only in touch with him now and again through Social Media Central. Seriously, we all tried different topics, but somehow this would lead to moments as awkward as those dreams where you suddenly find yourself naked.

Felicity worked the crowd, genuinely fascinated by what made these traitors tick. Shaun had a dreamy-eyed fetus of a girl attached to him for the night. In fact, she was so young, Felicity couldn't be jealous if she tried. And with his account still frozen, Shaun hadn't been seeking material for his profile on Lover Net blog.

"Tayler, I asked you what else is bothering you."

"Two things don't add up. Well, maybe the first one does."

Candy leaned forward.

"Okay, I'm annoyed that my friends have allowed this to happen."

"Allowed what to happen?"

"This." I gestured toward the crowd. "It's bad enough these people backstabbed them only a week ago, and now they're making amends. And the worst thing is, Madi, Connor, and Shaun are going along with it."

"Maybe they had no choice?"

"We all have a choice. Theirs is just a bad one."

"Then why are you here?"

I watched Madi try to be the belle of the ball. "I'm here for her."

Candy took note of who I was watching then placed her hand on my shoulder. "I think your friends are still scared about what happened and are just trying to regain status."

"But Social Media Central is their friend again. Well, they still can't log in, but their followers are being nice once more."

"But that's your point. They're two-faced. Your friends are just trying to strengthen their relationship with their fickle public."

I shook my head.

"What else is bothering you?" she asked.

"This crowd."

Candy glanced at them, shrugged, and then turned back to me.

"No one's taking drugs. No one's getting excessively drunk, and they're engaged in conversation."

"Well, people have lost a little of their interest in Social Media Central since you guys instigated Movie Night, even though they've created a dedicated review section for films where people can nominate who in their lives should watch them."

"No, that's not it." I pointed to the thing waddling around with Madi. "That's our crowd. Clueless. Primitive. Easily lead." I pointed to a brooding gent with hair so shiny he could create an oil slick just by swimming in the ocean. "And like most of the people here, he's sophisticated, well-groomed, and wears an expression that reeks of intelligence. He's not our crowd. Which makes me suspect that somewhere our real followers are still two-faced, secretly bitching about us on Social Media Central."

"Mike says hello," said Felicity. She had popped over to talk to us.

"Who's Mike?" Candy asked.

"An author whose book launch we attended," I replied. "Felicity owns the bookstore it was held at."

"A bookstore? They still exist?"

"Well, mine's taken off, thanks to Tayler and his buddies, regardless of the recent bad publicity," Felicity replied. "I now have three bookcases full of titles, thanks to them."

"Congratulations," said Candy. "Sorry, Felicity, I never thought to ask you what you did when I met you earlier."

"None of us ever do. Hell, most of us work online. Who really cares what SMC office we log onto?"

"What do you do, Candy?" I asked.

"I work as a personal assistant."

"For whom?"

"A social media wannabe who wants to be as big as you, Tayler."

I felt my cheeks go red. "I'm only big by association."

"I don't think you have any idea how well you're known," Candy replied. "In fact, you should be prouder of Movie Night than you are."

"Why?"

"There's a new consciousness brewing, thanks to you being the antihero."

"Me?" I think my cheeks got redder.

"Have you heard of the Life Experience Mob?" Candy asked.

"No," I replied.

"I have," Felicity said. "A customer mentioned them the other day. Apparently, they're taking reconnection one step further."

"How?"

"They're getting money together to build a place where the public can experience things," Candy replied.

"But there are parks for people to sit in," I said. "They can experience nature just by leaving their apartments."

"Felicity, Tayler, do you remember schools?"

We both nodded.

"I don't. This new company will give you the chance to experience a day at school. They're going to attempt a day at the beach."

"I heard they're going to try some historical things, too," Felicity said. "They're going to attempt a medieval banquet."

"See, Tayler, you're the injection the Social Media Socialites needed." She took a glass of champagne from a passing waiter's tray and raised it. "To social awareness through motion pictures."

We drank.

"Are these Life Experience people contactable on SMC?" I asked.

Candy shook her head. "They're staying underground, I've heard. I'll tell you more in just a moment."

"Why?" Felicity asked.

"I need to pee." Candy quickly frolicked into the mass, her urgency apparent.

"She's a good influence," said Felicity.

"Yeah. She made me feel important just for being me. I haven't felt that way since, oh, it doesn't matter."

"It must matter if you brought it up."

"No, it's silly. I have Madi and Connor and you and Shaun."

"And you have someone new."

"True." I pulled out my device and found a selfie with me, Madi, Connor and Candy. "This was taken by Candy just after she showed up as we were sitting outside Connor's apartment. She insisted on it and uploaded to prove Madi and Connor's innocence. Madi joked that it would be the most famous selfie she ever took." I put my device away. "I think we'll be friends long after she goes home."

"Everyone connects on a different level, Tayler."

I watched Madi with her unwelcome attachment. "I relate to Candy. Her parents are on a different plane to her, just like mine are. Her parents weren't as bad as mine, but..."

"Go on."

"No, it's silly. I'm wallowing in self-pity."

"Your emotions matter. Now, wallow."

I smirked. "I never felt my parents were there. I mean, they were there, but they weren't there for me. Sure, they posted things about me a lot, but by the time I was toddler, they took center stage in all their selfies while I meandered in the background." I smirked once more. "But Audrey was *really* there for me."

"Your first girlfriend?"

"No, my fourth-grade teacher. She taught me the value of me. Even when I was home with my preoccupied parents, I still felt I was special thanks to Audrey. Somehow, I lost that after school went totally online through SMC."

"Well, now you have Candy, even if she does live outside of Astra City. She's given you a sense of self again that's unique from what Madi, Connor, Shaun, or I can give you. Don't lose that feeling." She looked at the crowd. "Have you noticed how pubescent that girl with Shaun is?"

"He looks bored. Which is odd because I've never known Shaun to get bored with anyone."

"She's salivating over him like he's a roast dinner. And he's busy trying to chat to everyone else."

"Why don't you join him?"

"You know, normally I would, but the people here are truly interesting. Did you handpick a rented crowd online?"

I chuckled. "I don't think I could have found a crowd this vibrant online."

"What are you guys talking about?" asked Connor. He had strolled up with his date. I couldn't answer without implicating his weird invitee as one of the interesting guests.

"How's your mum, Stafford?" I asked instead.

Connor stared at me blankly while Felicity sported a wicked smile behind his back.

"She thinks I should be a priest," Stafford replied.

"Do they still exist in Astra City?" I asked.

"Of course. Father Steve is a personal friend of mine."

"Who is Father Steve?"

"What do you mean, *Who is Father Steve*?"

"I've been asking that question all night," Connor confessed.

"Search me," said Felicity.

"Why, he's the Father to end all Fathers." Stafford huffed in contempt. "He's the ultimate Father."

"Sounds like a father figure," I said.

Stafford waved his arms about as if he was having an epileptic fit. "Connor, your friends are ignorant. They may be famous, but they're ignorant. I'm going back to that beauty-pageant winner we were talking to earlier. Are you coming?"

"I'll stay here and talk to my ignorant friends," he replied.

Stafford stormed off toward Madi and her strawberry-clad admirer.

"When was Madi in a beauty pageant?" I asked.

"Not her," Connor explained. "The woman with her."

"She was in a beauty pageant?"

"Apparently, back in the day."

As Stafford approached Madi, she shot a glance our way. I returned her plea for help with a naïve look.

"You know, I ask myself every day why I'm single. Then I meet guys like Stafford and praise the gods I'm single. What is it about this city that attracts screwball gay guys?"

"Can I be blunt?" I asked.

"Yes."

"I've never seen you date."

"That's true," said Felicity. "You always have a camera in your hand. It's like an extension of your body. It's your calling card to flirt. But you never date."

"And because tonight you're without your attachment, you're not sure how to connect with anyone," I commented.

"Sorry, did you not realize what a fruitcake my date is?" Connor scratched his head as if he were getting rid of dandruff.

"But look who else is here," said Felicity. "There are heaps of sexy men all waiting to be held captive by the Connor charm."

"She's right," I said.

"Hell, you don't even realize when someone is coming on to you," Felicity added.

"That's true." I looked Connor straight in the eye. "You'll flirt with camera in hand, but if someone makes the first pass, you're oblivious."

"Take those dark glasses off for once and really notice who's out there." Felicity mimed this action, flinging her imaginary glasses into the crowd.

"Prince Charming is waiting, but not in the dark." I held my hand to my heart as I gazed whimsically at the guests.

"I can't take off these glasses," he said. "They're prescription."

"But they make you look like a poser," said Felicity. "Sorry, Connor, but they do."

"And look at our crowd tonight," I said. "They're a classy bunch."

"You noticed that too?" he asked.

"You're Connor, aren't you?" asked the barman. He was a wet dream in a waistcoat. He adjusted his checked tie, loosening it for comfort. "Of course you are. What a stupid question."

"There are no stupid questions," Connor said. "Only stupid answers."

But after that moment of bravado, Connor looked back to us in order to continue our conversation. Felicity scowled at him, while I turned to the potential Romeo.

"Sir, can you get Connor to lend a hand?" the barman asked me.

He was cutting limes with an odd knife. Its handle looked like an extended tooth. An odd butter-yellow tooth.

Felicity's face contortions must have worked.

Shyly, Connor entered his workspace and pointed to the knife. "Where did you find a knife with an ivory handle?"

"A what?" I blurted.

"It's an antique knife with a handle made from ivory. The practice was banned before our time. They'd kill animals, such as elephants, just to make cutlery."

The mystery man handed Connor the implement and then looked to us with a sly grin. We took the hint. We moseyed away, only to see Stafford charging in our direction.

"How does this make me look?" he said to us. "Social Media Central will be full of pictures with Connor and his unofficial date."

"Who's taking pictures?" I said. "I haven't seen anyone who's device-obsessed here."

"Can't you just find someone else?" Felicity said. "What does it matter, really? Who's going to care?"

"The public," Stafford replied. "The damned public!"

"But no one's taking pictures," I said again. "See. Not one selfie. Not one picture." I stepped away from this idiot.

"Where are you going?" Felicity pleaded. She displayed an oversized smile behind his back. "Stafford needs support. He feels jilted." It's amazing how sincere she sounded.

"Felicity, Stafford, I'm sympathetic. Honestly, I am, but I need to pee. I promise I'll be right back."

With a voice of a strangled cat, Stafford kept making accusations of Connor's unfaithfulness. Felicity looked as bored as a blind guy watching a silent movie. But beyond them, Connor was caught in an engaged conversation, captivated by a barman he should've photographed.

I escaped through the maze of dapper chaps and chic flappers. As I passed, many acknowledged me with a wink or a raised glass. I returned their greetings with a warm smile.

"Let me see your screen," someone said.

"Huh?"

"What type of screen does the famous Tayler use?"

I pulled it out.

"I *knew* it." She called to a male with a painted mustache. "I won the bet." She grabbed my hand and lifted it and my device into the air. "It's snazzy!"

"What are you doing?"

She let go of me.

"That loser over there and I had a bet. He thought you'd still have one of those old-fashioned phone things, but I knew you'd have the latest technology."

"I did until recently, but they're closing down the old telephony network soon, so I had to upgrade. It's odd having to log into SMC just to make a call now, but I guess that's progress."

She reached into her handbag and pulled out a wafer-thin sheet. As she held it to my face, the light turned its frame from black to dark cherry red.

"This is *my* looking glass to the world. Sleek, isn't it?"

I have to confess, I was impressed. I couldn't care two hoots about the mindless content that SMC would display on its screen, but the design was true art. I took it from her. I could see my own admiration in the reflection from its silver screen.

"It's like a mirror," I muttered.

"Only when it's off. Here, let me turn it on. Tayler, on."

With those words, the all-too-well-known SMC logo made its presence felt.

"You called your device *Tayler*?"

"Can you think of a better name for the gadget that keeps me sane?"

"What do you mean?"

"It's how I keep you with me all the time. I tell it what to do and it listens to my commands, never letting me down. It sleeps with me. It wakes me up. It listens to my problems. It entertains me. It delights me. Let's face it, it's my best friend."

"What about movie night? Do you share cinema?"

"I watch movies. I don't share."

My bladder was reminding me of the very reason I'd left Felicity and the oddball. Somehow, I had found another who didn't fit in with this refined lot. I handed the extension of psychological solitude back to her and stepped away promptly.

Cocktails were now being served. Concoctions of many colors added delight to our guest's already cheerful faces. One couple stepped in front of me, inviting me to Charleston. Dizzy jazz with an electronic beat took over from the wistful instrumentals that had been played up until this point.

I shooed the couple aside gracefully, making them understand my need for relief. The male pointed toward the floor as a gesture to make sure I would come back and dance. *Why didn't this couple catch me a moment earlier for conversation?*

After I flushed the toilet, I noticed a murmur coming from the bathroom. I strolled down the hallway to investigate. A group of three people stood like statues in front of a glass bathtub. Between their bodies, I could see someone in the tub, so I stepped forward.

Dread weighed me down like an anchor the moment I saw the crimson slit on her throat. I too had turned to stone as I took in the mess of red splotches in her signature blue hair. And resting on her breast was that knife with an ivory handle, its glistening blade marked with blood and skin. *Is this a dream? Has the police's fantasy world become a reality?*

Candy did, however, seem at peace. Not that she was the intense type, but her bubbly nature was taking a rest. The personality she used to brighten our world in the last couple of days was simply recharging. *Yes, that's it! She's sleeping.* I didn't want her to be dead.

I was yanked away down the hall before I even knew I had left the crime scene. We scampered out of the apartment through a servant's entrance I had never known existed. Felicity was tugging my arm so hard I feared bruising, but Shaun led her toward our escape.

Outside, we stood with a couple of other guests who had followed. We heard bewildered chatter toward the front of the building, so we cautiously crept toward it. Shaun halted abruptly.

"What is it?" I whispered. But he didn't have to answer. Military men in black metal armor were forcing Madi and Connor into a van.

# Fourteen

"NO NEED FOR introductions," said Mary. She swooned as she welcomed Shaun and me into her apartment.

For the past hour, we had hidden inside a cab just outside the building, after bribing the driver to take us from the chaos of the Dames and Gangsters bash. He cleverly told us to lie on the back seat and threw a blanket over us. Although it was uncomfortable, leaning against Shaun calmed me. He breathed into the back of my neck, making me tingle within his aura.

Felicity wanted to come with us, but Shaun insisted she go home. She did, although reluctant, even though she totally understood her boyfriend's motives in trying to keep her well away from this dangerous lunacy.

We had just snuck up the back stairs to visit my landlady.

"I need to leave my key with you," I told her.

"Fugitives on the run, I take it."

"Has the news spread already?" Shaun asked.

"It's what we, the Amazing Three, have been chatting about all evening."

I quickly looked to her computer but saw no face on her monitor, just someone's profile page on Lover Net. I was as relieved as a runner who'd just hit the finish line.

"So, you're the Amazing Three now?" I was half-curious.

"Bernard caught me cheating."

"You mean you actually visited the other one?"

"Cassidy."

"Yes, Cassidy. You got to cheat with a man more than half your age. Go Mary!"

"No, I only did a little dirty talk during a mirror meal." She lowered her head. "He's a better cook than me. His stir-fry looked so vibrant, the beans nearly jumped out of my screen."

"So you cheated by merely flirting?"

"Flirting is still cheating."

"I did a whole blog on this," Shaun said. "Lovers Net is full of flirts one step away from cheating."

"Huh?"

Mary nodded as if what he said made perfect sense, so I had to change the subject.

"Mary, what is the latest news about us?"

"You're all suspects. Even you two."

"We are?" Shaun queried.

"Are you sure?"

"Social Media Central have identified you and Shaun and the other two—"

"You mean Madeline and Connor."

"Yes, the suspicious-looking ones. I was just saying what a good person you were to Cassidy and Samantha, as they wanted to know all about you."

"What did you say?"

"That they already have the guilty locked up. I mean, they confessed. What do they need you for?"

Shaun seemed panicked, but then I realized I felt the same. I rushed to her dusty computer and searched for the names of my arrested companions. There they were, trending, but not in ways that would make their mothers proud. Many sites reported their admission to murder, yet at no point did I see a video of the actual confession.

And some mentioned that ivory knife, with a few badly taken snaps of Connor cutting limes with the murder weapon. But I didn't see anyone taking photos at the party. The upward angle of these pics suggested a sneaky photographer.

"Type in our names," Shaun instructed.

I did. The police wanted to talk to us, yet no official section of SMC mentioned why. Of course speculation ran rampant in private posts. One referred to me as "the clueless accomplice" and another as "Failure Tayler." My passionate buddy was referred to as "show-pony Shaun" or "lady-killer," the latter for all the wrong reasons.

An icon appeared, bursting with color at the side of the display. I clicked its aggravating logo. Soon the page where the public could submit their verdict popped up. The court case had not only been resurrected, it was live. All of this would have been laughable if it wasn't so ludicrous.

"I'm going to the police," I declared.

"Are you mad?" Shaun asked.

"Yes I am, but someone's got to sort out this insanity. The public are getting out of hand thanks to the authorities, and I need to get to the bottom of this."

"But what if they lock you up?"

"Then I'll be with Madi and Connor. Aren't you even the least bit curious to know where they are?"

Shaun slumped against one of Mary's grayish walls. "Sorry. Of course, you're right. This whole thing is not helping me think straight. I had my mind on Felicity."

"I see." I reached into my pocket and pulled out my keys. "Here, Mary. You'll need to feed your own cats."

"I can't," she said. "I'm going on a holiday."

"Wherever to?"

"To America and Switzerland."

"Whatever for?"

"Cassidy's in America, and Samantha is in Switzerland."

"Cassidy didn't have a hint of an American accent. Besides, how can you afford the trip?"

"I'm not paying for it." She gave me a wise woman's wink.

"Mary, did you win one of those 'Meet Your Friends' lotteries?"

"No, Cassidy and Samantha are chipping in."

I felt my face distort. "You don't know these people."

"Yes I do. They're my true friends."

"Mary, you're old enough to remember a time I never knew. A time when Astra City wasn't an oversized ghost town of glass and steel. You used to tell me about eating at a restaurant or a café when you first arrived here. Some people even left their home to meet their friends face to face. Remember those friends we used to have dinner with? I wish we could return to those days.

"Hopefully, soon, those idiots that follow me, Shaun, Madi, and Connor will pick up a book instead of their screens. They'll discuss the fantastic tales that authors wrote a century or two ago, instead of just finding a connection through Movie Night. Maybe plays will be performed again. Maybe concerts will be held." I rubbed my bristled chin. "Hey, call me romantic, but imagine those fools genuinely going on a date that leads to the bedroom for the type of encounter that can't be found through staring at a screen."

I turned to Shaun to gauge his reaction, but he crouched in the corner as lost as an orphan boy. Yet a moment before, he'd been my private hero in the back seat of a taxi, making me feel safe just because he was as familiar as worn jeans.

"If we stay here, we'll be arrested," I said.

"But who'll feed my cats?"

"Mary, they're your responsibility." I grabbed her hand and slapped my keys in her palm. "And if somehow you do end up in the northern hemisphere, make sure Cassidy doesn't turn you into his sex slave." I winked and then laughed. "Shaun, I *am* going to the police. You really should work out what you want to do. This sounds cruel, but if you go into hiding, perhaps you shouldn't let Felicity know where you are, for her sake."

# Fifteen

THAT SAME POLICEWOMAN who had interviewed me the week before ran to me as soon as I entered the station. Her cohorts seemed tempted to do the same, but as she dashed past them, they shared their attention between me and their work screens, as if pretending not to notice an attractive member of the opposite sex.

I still made eye contact with some. One older cop observed me in a manner that creeped me out. Another younger man grinned foolishly as I passed, as if he desperately wanted to ask for my autograph.

"I'm glad you're here, Tayler," said my escort. But that's not what the tone of her voice seemed to say. She sounded like an employee about to knock off, until her boss staggered her with a mountain of data entry duties.

We left the front office, my back jolting at the many stares shooting into my spine. I was relieved to close the door behind me.

"You're not saying much."

"That's an understatement. I haven't *said* anything."

"What's on your mind?"

"Everything and nothing, all at the same time."

"Why did you come here?"

"It seems I'm a suspected accomplice in a murder, or so Social Media Central is saying." I stopped in my tracks. "Why did you ask me that?"

"What do you mean?"

"You'd know I was wanted for questioning. You wrote a blog about it!"

She stood, serene.

"Oh, whatever. I don't know what to think anymore. It's time for us to talk and try to work this whole thing out. Trust me, I have many questions to ask."

Her face had no expression.

"Are Madeline Q and Connor here?"

"They're safe."

"But are they here?"

She pointed. "Go into that room. I promise we'll get to the bottom of this."

I sighed before ambling toward the door. The scent of my own deodorant pleased me. I gazed downward at my jeans. My favorite pair. Faded and softened through many shared experiences. I might have been slightly delirious, but I was so glad Mary convinced me to shower and change before I got there.

I looked up as I entered the interview room to find a familiar face on the other side of the table. He stood and held out his hand.

"Tayler, it's good to see you again."

At first, I didn't remember where I'd met him. *Is he an older fan who caught my eye once? Is he one of Mary's cyberlovers who I happened to see on her screen when I placed money on her table?* But I then noticed the burgundy coat hanging on the back of his chair. Reality hit.

"The man in the park," I said, my voice unsteady. I meekly shook his hand and took a seat. He sat confidently.

"My name is Stuart, remember? Although to some I'm known as the Government."

"You're the government?"

"Surely you've seen my face somewhere ruling the country."

I think my jaw dropped.

"See, your generation doesn't even know who's in power. In fact, so many people these days don't take notice of me."

"You used to pay me a wage."

"Until things got out of hand."

"Stuart, I'm too tired to argue—"

"Refer to me as the Government. I prefer it."

The hairs on my neck rose. "I have questions."

He nodded.

"Where's Madi and Connor?"

"They're safe. I can take you to them if you want." He checked his device. "Actually, I'll take you to them soon. They're dining at the moment."

"But it's late. It's close to midnight."

"You've never heard of a midnight snack?"

I swallowed hard. "I have so many questions."

"Then ask them."

"How can Madi and Connor be guilty of murder? In fact, how could they be guilty of murder twice, when the first time there wasn't even a body?"

"You'll have to ask them. They confessed."

"Okay, let's pretend that they've confessed—"

"We don't need to pretend. They have."

"Okay, but how could they be guilty of the murder of someone as wonderful as Candy simply from a photograph she posed for in a bathtub. I mean, she was alive somewhere living her life, so obviously the police didn't have a body. And now—"

"They thought they did."

"No one ever thinks they have a body when they haven't. It's beyond ridiculous. And Candy deserved better!"

"Tayler, your emotions are getting in the way of asking the questions you really want to ask."

"Okay then. Why have we been framed?"

"Framed? Tut-tut. Such an accusation. Didn't you read about the knife?"

"An ivory-handled knife that someone handed to Connor to cut limes. Instantly, we know of two sets of fingerprints and DNA on the murder weapon. There's bound to be more. There's bound to be one particular set belonging to a cleverly planted murderer that blended in with the stylish set of guests who barely resembled the losers who come to our parties." I gritted my teeth. "So, I ask again. It's a simple question, even for you. Why have we been framed and why did Candy have to die just for *your* revenge?"

He said nothing, yet his steady stream of breath blew on my face. He then rose, pacing casually along the opposite wall. Next, he halted and peered at me.

"You haven't answered me, Government."

"*The* Government, if you please."

"Stuart, this is nonsense. Your silence equals guilt. I have more questions that need answering, like where the hell are Madi and Connor?"

"You're right, dear Tayler, you're so right. Where are my manners? I should show you where your friends are. But I need you to wear a blindfold while my driver takes us to them."

"No. I don't trust you. Not after what happened to—"

"But we had such a good rapport in the park that day."

"Why were you in that park that day? Were you there specifically to meet me?" I began to feel clammy. I looked at my right palm and, for some reason, examined my lifeline.

"What's the matter?"

"Stuart—"

"No. The Government."

I shot up, wanting to charge at him like a jailbird with a grudge. "Stuart, stop wasting my time. Where are Connor and Madeline?"

"Blindfold, Tayler. I'm afraid you haven't got a choice."

"I can go back home."

"But you're a suspected accomplice. It's all over Social Media Central."

I licked my bottom lip.

"Besides, I know Madeline Q is dying to see you." He kept talking as he escorted me back through the main office, although I didn't really listen. I was a man starting at the first square of a board game, where every roll of the dice would change my fate. But this board game had an echo. The reverberating voices of the characters I had met in the past months felt neither near nor far. And soon, I was drifting with these voices until the black limousine appeared, waiting in that lonely night.

Common sense told me not to go with him. If a funky out of towner ended up giving her life to frame my friends, then what chance had I of surviving this night? But if Madi or Connor could still be saved, then I would never forgive myself if I didn't at least try to rescue them. As I climbed in, the million and one scenarios racing around in my head stopped me from thinking clearly.

Stuart handed me a mauve blindfold he'd pulled from the pocket of his coat. As I took it, he raised three fingers to the driver. His chauffeur tilted his head, his ghostly figure hidden by his cap and jacket.

The vehicle purred as the sharp sound of intermittent cars zipped past like comets. Transport was a foreign sound in my neighborhood. A baritone voice teased me with fragments of a conversation during our one traffic stop. The bizarre vibration that told pedestrians to walk ricocheted from abandoned buildings as if it was a Martian laser gun from a vintage sci-fi flick. And the damn air-conditioning was set to antarctic, freezing me like leftovers.

We slowed down. Halves of a metal gate slid apart, rattling in stereo. An unearthly female spoke, welcoming my man of riddles. We drove on. We stopped. My door creaked as it opened, allowing the natural cool air to warm me.

I stumbled to my feet as Stuart spoke in his smooth tone, guiding me with his hand in mine. Another moving object reverberated from left to right, before all I heard was the hum of a screen.

"You can take your blindfold off now."

I did. Glaring at me was an oversized display showing the voting results of the citizen jurors. Punters had examined the evidence and were madly playing with the lives of my friends. And it wasn't looking good.

"It's all a bit of theater, Tayler. And you know how much the public like their entertainment."

"How can the public be so easily led?"

"In my youth, I saw the last remnants of religion. Sure, some still practice their desired faith, and Astra City has a church or two hiding somewhere, but they're solo acts in an age of reason. And reason dictates that a new following has to be invented for the masses. We supply the event. They supply their faith."

"Where's Madi and Connor?"

"In time, Tayler. In time."

The light from the screen danced on Stuart's face like video artwork. He, himself, part of this surreal experience, with me the observer, affected by many emotions. The hallmark of any great work of a creative soul.

"It's all smoke and mirrors, isn't it? And the Government has hidden himself within the framework."

"You are clever. But the real sign of intelligence is how much of this you can work out."

"I can see how. But you're still making me grapple with why."

A servant in a black robe wandered in from a side door, leaving it ajar. He seemed as old as me. His spotless bald head had been meticulously shaved by a razor. Rectangular turquoise glasses framed his eyes, the color mirrored in the detailed tattoo that crept up his arm. Faces from past generations stared from the windows of Astra City buildings, a snapshot of history captured on his skin. But what were these people concerned about? What was the change that they foresaw?

He held out a tray with two glasses of red wine. He grinned.

"Number Thirteen is quite the character, don't you think? He likes fun as much as he likes men his own age."

At first, I didn't feel it, but I'm sure it was triggered in the pit of my gut. As I reached for the glass, the rage strengthened. I picked up the stem and threw the wine in Stuart's face. Then I ran for the open door.

An electric charge pulsed through me. My body wanted to explode. My ears rang, but the sound quickly faded with my vision. Someone's breath cooled my damp cheek, and as I fought to regain my sight, I lost my grip on consciousness.

# Sixteen

"Tayler, are you awake?" It was Madi's voice. My eyelids flicked open, and she kissed every inch of my face.

"Let him breathe, Madeline," Connor murmured. He stood against the bars of our cell.

"Hey, at least our prison is clean," I said.

And it was, even down to the chair I was slumped on. Shiny metal rods pressed cold against my back. And the bones in my ass craved a cushion.

Wherever we were, this was the only cell. All we could see was a hallway leading to a singular door, again metallic. We had a sink and, to my relief, a toilet in a separate room within our confines.

My companions were still in their costumes from the party. Connor's waistcoat was slightly ripped, and Madi's eloquent gray dress resembled a tacky hand-me-down.

"So why have we been framed?" I asked.

"Movie Night," Connor replied.

"Seriously? I was the one who promoted Movie Night. Yet *you* were the ones taken by the police."

"While you're locked up with us now, which proves my point. I'm sure you were hiding when the cops burst in on the party."

My head slumped.

"Face it, we're all being punished for the things we said, some of it during the live stream. We're the baddies who encouraged people to connect face to face. Good little socialites don't stray off message."

"And you really believe it has nothing to do with certain political aspirations?"

He stared at me for a moment. "How would the Government know about my thoughts of taking his role? Sure, we joked around on Shaun's blog, but I was only serious in private messages."

"On the all-encompassing, all-knowing Social Media Central." I sat back. "You've said some silly things, Connor. Remember your crack about our food being grown in a laboratory."

"But it is!"

"But you didn't need to say it."

"Regardless, that's no reason to commit state-sanctioned murder."

I swallowed loud enough to scare birds from their branches. "The Government is a madman, you know."

Their eyes widened.

"Sorry, of course you know. You've spent some time with him." I ran my hand up and down one of the cold metal rods on the back of my chair. "All I wanted was people united through experience, even if they had to watch a screen for a while to instigate it. It was great to see the rebirth of communication. And you're right, Connor. That's hardly a reason to kill an innocent fan and hang us out to dry."

"Yes, it is, Tayler. How can the Government control the flock if the people are not within his reach?" Connor shivered, uncharacteristically. "Who am I kidding? My political aspirations were the icing on the cake."

"Don't beat yourself up. I'm in here too. My girlfriend is here—"

Madi cleared her throat. "Connor, I know you," she said. "In the back of that clever mind is a man who toys with ideas he becomes serious about."

He opened his mouth, but no words fell out. Madi crouched beside me, pushed my chin up with her finger, and caressed my cheekbone with her thumb.

"No, Madi," I said, "we're all in here. Connor's right. It's about all of us equally." I felt my eye water. "Oh dear, Shaun."

"What about Shaun?"

"They'll want him too because of the online banter about Connor wanting to lead Astra City. Plus he promoted Movie Night. Erotic films were being shared face to face, leading to contact." My hand pressed against Madi's thumb on my cheek. "What will Stuart do next? Find a way to hypnotize everyone through their mobile devices and turn us into androids?"

Connor laughed. "Possibly. He doesn't want us to be human."

"Your minds are so random, guys," said Madi.

"There's method in our madness," I said. "We invented our future masters over a century ago."

"Say what?"

"Computers. They now control us, and we're a generation who doesn't know better."

"Tayler, my screen is my companion. It listens to me," Madi said.

"Does it?" Connor asked. He began pacing. "Madeline, remember how you could concentrate on an SMC video for a couple of minutes when you were young?"

She nodded.

"Then the discussion boards debated whether thirty seconds was the best length for any video on the net. Your screen has shortened your attention span. That's not what a good companion does to you."

"What about movies?" Madi reasoned. "They're a lot longer than thirty seconds."

He halted, standing directly in front of us. "Tayler likes old movies. Hey, some you like aren't even in color."

"So?"

"Those classics seem to run forever, but a modern film is roughly forty-five minutes to an hour. And even then, people talk through them or have to watch them twice. So, Tayler, how often do you watch the same film to take in the whole plot?"

"Older films aren't as fast-moving," I replied. "So I relax and notice the little things, like the costumes or the sets. And I read up on the making of the film while I watch."

"Yet, when they were made, there were no personal computing devices."

"Well, however they watched them. They stopped the video and took a break," said Madi.

"No, my love, he's right. They watched them in cinemas, from start to finish."

"Cinemas?"

"A large room with a huge screen in front of the audience."

"Didn't they get bored?"

"No," Connor replied. "They could concentrate for a lot longer."

"So, what's your point?"

"The Government wants us to retain less and less. Well, not you, me, or Tayler. We were the bait. But for the rest of society, it's been slowly happening for generations."

"We're prisoners of a madman, and you're giving a lecture on concentration spans. Way to go, Connor."

"Madi, seriously, don't you see it? By creating a daily social event around us, the masses were shown something new all the time, which was then amplified through the many points of view of our followers, which, as we can see with this silly murder business, is then mistaken for the truth. They're overloaded with content so they can't get bored easily, or scrutinize what they've been told before. And now, when they're without Social Media Central, they're lost. They don't know how to entertain themselves or analyze the information they've been given. They're robotic drones."

"Both of you are not making sense. Why would the Government want a society of robotic drones? And they're not drones. We've met our public. They're not the classiest bunch, but they're not lifeless."

"But they don't think for themselves," said Connor. "They have personalities, but no character. And even then, their personalities are reduced to social profiles. In a digital world where everything is on tap, who needs real life? Real life is too slow for modern minds. In fact, does real life even exist anymore?"

Madi thought for a bit. "My fashion was real. My outfits were real."

"We were the lucky ones," said Connor. "We were allowed to have a life. All governments need compliant citizens, not rebels. But then *we* rebelled. That was not the example we were supposed to display."

"It's funny," I said. "In old movies, people would take long lunch breaks. Hell, the fact that they took an hour for lunch at all is surprising. Sometimes, I've seen them go back to work drunk, and their fellow workers just laugh."

"Seriously?" Madi queried. "What has that got to do with anything?"

"Once upon a time, the workplace was human. Civilization was human. Now it's an efficient machine with every part focused on what he or she has to do. Our fans have jobs. Their ancestors had careers. And I was one of the mindless androids working harder and more efficiently."

"Then you joined us in becoming someone to amuse the public," said Connor. "To dumb them down, if you like. The Government still doesn't want them to think, whether it's through movies or through my so-called political ideas."

"I still think you're way off the mark," said Madi. "The truth is, none of us really know what the Government is up to."

"You're wrong. We know he couldn't control us anymore, so he had to discredit us."

"Should we be talking about this openly in this cell?" I asked. "There's a good chance we're being spied on."

We huddled together.

"And what about Candy?" Madi whispered.

"Collateral damage," Connor replied.

"But the whole plan was stupid from the start," I said. "I mean, they set her up by photographing her here in Astra City. Small-town girl gets a chance to travel to the big smoke. Then they use that photo to create a fake murder case. It's so uninspired, it's laughable. How did the Government think it would not be uncovered?"

"Yet, regardless of a murder that didn't happen and now did, the punters are still voting. Like I said, our public are mindless drones."

"Maybe the voting is rigged, just like the evidence."

"There's evidence?" Madi asked.

"Apparently you've both confessed, and—"

"What is it, my love?"

"I saw her body. Throat slit. Bloodstains. And that ivory-handled knife planted on her breast. It would be laughable if it wasn't so tragic. B-grade setup all the way."

Madi looked away while Connor faced the back wall.

"Then why isn't anyone saying anything?" she asked.

"They probably are, but their comments are being deleted," Connor replied. "Plus, everyone is talking to smaller and smaller groups of people. It takes a long time for a mass counterargument to evolve."

I smirked. "What you're saying reminds me of my landlady, Mary. Her circle of Social Media Central friends keeps shrinking. Their discussions about your guilt became as private as ours here in this cell."

"But *we* had a huge following," said Madi.

"Yes, we had a huge *following*," Connor replied. "They weren't our friends. They just wanted to be us. Seriously, how often did you respond to any of them?"

"We were the content," I said. "Packaged in glossy paper as a distraction to their humdrum lives. Now they've got a court case to get excited about, as real as the sham that was our celebrity."

"Ouch," uttered Madi. "But there's got to be someone who's paying attention and thinking this through."

"SMC works on algorithms," Connor said. "Content shows up on a person's screen depending on what words they type in their posts, or what keywords they add to its mighty search engine. Their interests are shared by the all-knowing being, and it alone decides what to share with that individual. Perhaps it censors as well."

"Like I said before, we invented our master over a century ago."

"You're both sounding creepy," said Madi.

Butterflies darted wildly in my stomach. I had to sit down. I ignored the lone chair and gradually eased my way to the floor. I nestled my head between my knees. As I shut my eyes, Candy's mischievous face flickered in my mind.

In the short week we'd known each other, I had admired her small-town charm. She had a vitality quite different from those of us in our lonely towers.

She'd once described her family home as half-transitioned. I told her I didn't get her meaning, so she explained that her parents were finally earning enough money to modernize the house left to them from her grandparents.

They replaced a wall of collectible art with a state-of-the-art screen. Each bedroom had its own screen, supplanting the antique bookshelves and furniture. She had a soft spot for a particular teapot she'd saved from the rubbish heap. It had been handed down through generations and, in her opinion, had a life force of its own.

Through her childhood, it appeared in her dreams. Not often, but enough times to make its presence felt. One night, it expanded like a balloon until it was large enough to be her carriage. She stepped inside and showered the townsfolk with gold coins.

As I'd listened, I longed to be taken on wild rides in my slumber. Nothing even close to that vision had ever entered my head during the night. *Has my imagination been robbed by screens?*

Candy shared the same fear, so she'd spoken up against the renovations in her family home. After a few more modern touches, her parents had finally taken note and stopped robbing the house of its essence. She even insisted that new shelving be put up next to the main screen so that collectibles could stand proudly once more.

"Where are you, Tayler?" Madi asked.

"In my happy place."

My eyelids flicked open at the sound of the door opening down the hall. Number Thirteen marched toward us, typing madly on his small screen. The door to our cell made a buzzing sound. Its low hum was somehow relaxing. He placed the gadget in his pocket with one hand and drew a gun with the other. Possibly the same gun that had sent a charge through my body during our last meeting. Now our cell door slowly opened.

He pointed the weapon at Madi and me and gestured for us to follow. We did as he casually walked backward. But then Connor rushed him. Number Thirteen fired. Connor screamed and then lay as lifeless as a rag doll on the floor.

# Seventeen

"It's late."

"No, it's early," Stuart said to me. "I'd say it's sometime after two a.m."

More metal dominated this minimalist nightmare. Thankfully, exotic food splashed color on the soulless table. Iridescent green beans and a mountain of mashed potato had been placed near my end. A chocolate cake with raspberry icing running down its side sat near Madi.

But we hadn't touched the food. I was too scared of what might have been in it. I also feared Number Thirteen and his electric gun, both watching over us like hawks.

And again, to our side, was another screen tallying up the never-ending results of the bogus murder case. I wasn't shocked that the guilty verdict was still higher than common sense.

"Why aren't you eating?" Stuart said, chewing in spin cycle.

"You just killed Connor!" I replied.

"Oh, you poor haunted soul. Connor's not dead. Not yet. I have a use for him."

"But I saw—"

"You saw a man knocked unconscious, just as you were earlier. He'll wake in an hour or two."

Madi picked up a bean and crunched. In three bites, it was gone.

"Why are you feeding us?" I asked.

"Someone has to."

"But you told me Madi and Connor had dinner."

"No, I didn't."

"Yes, you did, at the police station. You said they were having a midnight snack."

"Do you believe everything I tell you, Tayler?"

"Then why not feed Connor now?"

"He thinks too much."

"I think just as much as Connor."

"But all you ever do is come up with questions. Connor comes up with answers."

"Well, in that case, I have a question for you..."

Madi sat like a nun in prayer. Not a word to say. Silent contemplation in her place.

"What's your question, Tayler?"

"Why did you put me on the payroll?"

"You were an experiment." He extended his arm to his side with his fork still in his hand. "You were somewhere out there. A thinker. An analyzer. The audience that steers away from the crowd."

"So, I was recruited."

"You catch on quick once you're given the right clues." He looked to Madi, but her head was lowered, unaware of his gaze. "You were our loner model. You represented the ones who aren't swayed by glitter, glamour, or sex. We couldn't ask for a perfect pairing."

"And did you succeed in dumbing down the people you were trying to reach?"

"I don't need to answer that. You know we did. You met your fans."

"So, was it Movie Night or Connor's joke about ruling that caused you to commit murder?"

"Tut-tut. Manners, please. That's not the way to address your host."

"Okay, let's break this down, Stuart."

He gave me a death stare, which I ignored.

"Movie Night, of all things, would have appealed to the outsiders like me. By bringing me into the fold, you had a Trojan horse within your cyberwalls."

"Well, I must admit, it wasn't my idea to include you. One of my advisors thought it was worth the test so I tagged along. Silly, really. We already had other schemes brewing to guide the thoughts of the masses, but I gave in to his flight of fancy."

"But whatever you're up to, you'll still run into people like me. And you'll still run into people like Connor."

He placed blue vein on a cracker. "There'll always be rebels. That's what guided the internet decades ago. Lone wolves influencing opinion. Over time, we've been taking it back." He lay the delicacy on his plate. "In short, you and people like you are now yesterday's rebels. No voice. No influence."

"But rebels get rediscovered and others rise to fight their cause."

"But you're one rebel they're not listening to. You never did have a profile on Social Media Central. Such a shame. We hoped you would. You would have made an excellent quick-phrase. Little morsels of information from your keyboard would enlighten your lot, with our message thrown in for good measure. We did consider creating a fake account for you, but then we found we had to silence the Social Media Socialites. You cost too much."

I took my fork and ran it through a wad of mash. It tasted creamy—the type of creamy my landlady once knew how to master.

"Stuart, I may not be the rebel anyone's listening to, but there are others out there."

"And they'll play our tune when we unleash what we have planned."

He had to be bluffing. Still, it didn't stop my foot from tapping nervously.

"But whatever grand scheme you have up your sleeve, others will feel as disconnected as me."

"They'll weigh in, trust me. And we'll learn about them and what makes them tick as much as all the other idiots on SMC. We'll have the most accurate emotional blueprint of everyone in Astra City."

"But for you to learn about them, they'll have to share their feelings. How many people share things of real emotional value online? They talk in chunks."

"You've started the ball rolling with people sharing Movie Night. And seriously, what would you know about social media? You don't have a profile."

"That's beside the point. To me, you're going around in circles. One minute, you want to control what the people think. Another minute, you create celebrities to be your spokespeople. The next, you're getting off creating all-knowing files on every individual."

"One method didn't prove successful, so we're on to the next."

"A man with so many riddles can only end up a fool."

"Tayler, my dear boy, you think you're so clever."

Madi trembled, and then raised her head and smiled at him. It wasn't a smile of love, hope, or concern, but all three mixed together. The smile of a slave who wished for more but saw no way out. Stuart returned her gaze, looking older than his years.

I slumped as vomit shot up my throat. My girl raised herself like a ghost, floating without intent. But she had reason behind her lifeless eyes. She moved to him and slipped her leg over his lap. The Government grinned with too many teeth showing. He hadn't expected her to do this. I was sure of it.

She reached down and unzipped him. He slyly looked my way, sighing in that way only dirty old men know how.

"Madeline, a show for our guest?" he said. "How unexpected."

My arms stretched out to my sides of their own accord. I tried to howl, but no sound came out. Instead, I whimpered. My deflated tone was hardly audible, yet it reverberated through my submissive heart. I tried harder. If I was to regain sanity, I had to try harder. I roared.

"Well done, Tayler," said Stuart, snidely.

He raised his arms above his head and applauded me. At this point, Madi writhed with more rhythm, never shooting a glance my way.

I rose. He sat forward as Madi rode harder. I turned and glared at our tattooed guard. As he raised his gun, I strode toward him, full of self-assurance, yet without a plan. He extended his arm, the weapon now aimed squarely at my face. And then I licked my lips.

The gun lowered slightly. As my mouth met his, I heard it clang to the floor. And as we kissed, I longed for his moist tongue to lick a trail down my neck. I pushed his shaven head to my chest. He tasted my nipple after I raised my shirt. But I yearned to go down on him.

I crouched, unzipping his tight trousers. And as I reached inside with one hand, I picked up the gun with the other, aimed at his body, and pulled the trigger.

# Eighteen

I HEARD STUART commanding Madi to get off him. As for me, I was running for my life. I didn't have time to consider my mix of emotions on a deeper level. Words slipped through my mind instead. Betrayal. Lust. A thankful getaway.

Footsteps chased me through a maze of hallways. But I was much faster. What had to be an exit came into view. But nearby, I sensed the well-known hum of screens. Voices accompanied them, tidbits of conversation, alone, not making sense. Both the chatter and the exit were getting closer. I had a plan. Making as much noise as I could, I ran toward the metal doors, stamping my runners into the polished floor. To my disbelief, the doors slid open. I ran out, smiling at a dome on the ceiling that I realized had to house a camera.

Just as quickly, I halted and stepped back inside, trying to avoid the gaze of my silent videographer. Two men stood at a gate only several meters away. I pushed myself against the wall next to the open doorway. As the exit shut, I slid sideways and casually, yet silently, entered the room with the murmurs.

I was met by an attractive lady at a desk situated at the beginning of the longest hallway I'd ever seen. On either side was a series of doors, all in a row, disappearing into infinity.

"You're late, Smith." She typed something on a screen.

"Sorry."

"I can excuse lateness from our regulars, but from a newbie? What were you thinking?"

"I said I was sorry."

She tapped her fingers on the desk. "Well, I guess it is the early morning. And you do look tired. Perfect work for an insomniac." She stood. "Follow me."

Although my heart was pounding, I kept my cool. I strolled with her to an open doorway. The room inside was decked out like the living area of someone from the desperate end of town.

Mismatched sofas all out of shape faced a cardboard box posing as a coffee table, dirty mugs and a chocolate bar on its surface. Yet facing all of it was a modern computer and an intercom on a stainless-steel desk. And tucked into this modern furniture piece was an aged wooden chair with a broken back.

"There's a low-resolution camera fitted to the monitor. It will add to the illusion of your lack of wealth." She gestured toward the desk. "You remember your induction, don't you?"

I nodded and headed for the chair.

"Camden's details are in that folder so you can refresh yourself."

My gaze darted around.

"Next to the intercom, Smith. You have studied the notes we sent you?"

I grinned self-consciously.

"Wardrobe will be back shortly with clothes that fit your proposed status. Read up on your new pal in the meantime. We'll send a signal through his device shortly to wake him up."

She exited, her cold heels stamping the floor. On the top page inside the folder was an image of Camden. His olive skin and thick dark hair had me dreaming of travel in my exhausted state. Just him and me on a Greek island, sipping wine and soaking in sunshine. What an odd thought. I slapped my cheek and read his profile.

He was reaching out for new friends after being shunned by his old contacts on Social Media Central, and all for a mysterious reason. Something about the Inner Knowledge Net that he didn't want to join.

He believed his membership to this mysterious service was another way to control him. His mind had to be changed. This threw me. This was the first I'd heard of this section of SMC.

I lost my grip on the folder. A tall man returned with a crumpled T-shirt, so I fumbled on the floor, trying to pick up the files.

"This should be your size, Smith," he said. He laid it on the desk and winked. "Welcome to the team." He tottered around and browsed my fake decor. "What do you think? It's a bit down-market."

"Yeah, I guess."

He nodded. "But it serves its purpose. They've spent so much money on all these rooms and their fittings. It's a regular movie set, just for SMC." He paused. "Do I know you?"

I shook my head.

"Are you sure we've never met?"

"Nope."

He examined my face a moment longer. "Fair enough." He headed for the door. "Tayler! That's it. You look like Tayler. Has anyone told you that before?"

"I get it all the time."

"But I think you're better looking than him. Sad what's happening to him and his friends."

The intercom buzzed. "Camden's about to log on, Smith." It was that woman's voice. "You'll see his feed in a moment."

"I'd better go and leave you to it."

He shut the door promptly. All of a sudden, I understood the danger of my celebrity. I took off my glasses and pressed my hands into my hair in an effort to tame it. I never got to change into the T-shirt. There was only a moment's reflection on the screen to check myself before it turned itself on.

"I'm glad we're finally meeting," he said.

His winning smile could have seduced the most frigid human, and yet his voice had a sorrow I knew too well. That lonely resonance of being different because of a mind that questions everything.

"Hi, Camden."

"Hi, Smith."

*Smith? Is my supposed online identity also the name of my imposter self?*

"You look like that guy with the famous girlfriend."

"I get that a lot."

"Yeah, that loser. He'd be no one without that fashion blogger. Yet I can't understand this murder charge. What are the powers up to?"

"Search me," I said.

"I'm glad you contacted me," Camden said. "I couldn't sleep. Did you just get home from work?"

"Yes."

"That's why you're not too talkative. They should pay you better considering the hours you work."

"I know."

"Is Ogre Man still micromanaging you?" he asked.

"He's the worst. And that weird slobbering he does. It churns my stomach every night. He needs a servant with a rag chasing after him twenty-four seven."

"You never mentioned his slobbering before. Has he tried to crack onto you again?"

"No."

"What is it with midlife men? They think we're too poor to fight back."

There was only a white wall behind him with a poster peeling off it. That was my only hint to his world. I turned and checked my own dreary backdrop.

"We're slaves to our poverty," I said.

"True. But at least we have brains."

I tried to smile.

"Tell me about yourself, Smith."

"What haven't we talked about?"

"You've been coy about your sexuality."

"Perhaps I'm not sure myself, Camden."

"Really? I'm sure you're gay from what you've said."

"I think I'm bi."

"Then perhaps we'll date."

I felt myself blush.

"Hmm. Now I get why you're coy about your sexuality."

"Can we change the subject?"

"On one condition. The next time we get online, we mirror meal. You're cringing."

"The concept of sharing a meal in front of the screen is weird. I've done it once, and it felt stupid."

"That's strange. That's not what you've said before." Expression left his face. "Smith, remember that crackpot theory of mine? The one about the SMC employing psychologists posing as ordinary people?"

I shuddered. "That would make all our online relationships fake."

He stared past me. "How long have you had those couches?"

"Less time than you think."

"And your apartment?"

"The same." The door to my room slowly opened. That woman stood halfway in, peering like a cat with a mouse to molest. "What don't I know about you?"

"Well, I don't think I told you all about how my last set of friends deserted me."

"Go on."

"Have you heard of Inner Knowledge Net?"

I shook my head.

"All those other friends are on it, and when an ad came up on my screen demanding I should be a part of it, I questioned it with them. They didn't like my views."

"What is it?"

"The ad said it was my ticket to the 'in-crowd.' My ticket to success. Just log on, it said, and rewards await."

"Like what?"

"My own personal key to the secret section of SMC, with my own personal psychologist. Why I'd need one, I wasn't sure. Apparently, it would give me an edge over my other online friends. I think it's just another social conditioning tool. That's what I said to the others. Now they don't respond to me."

"Maybe it's safer to go with the flow these days."

That woman nodded.

"Actually, that's not really what I believe. We should start traveling outside our own walls," I added.

She frowned.

"Into our neighborhoods?" He winked.

"I was thinking outside of Astra City, but the streets would be a good start. They're deserted most of the time. At least the two of us would add some life to our neighborhood."

"What is there to do in this part of town? If I was stupid enough, I could've paid for tickets to swan around with that celebrity crowd. That would have been my 'in-crowd.' But even they're history. There's nothing except secluded nights indoors."

That woman left, leaving the door ajar.

"You have *me*. Is that so bad?"

"Let me ask you something, Smith. Expose your real self to me."

"What? Here?"

"Why not? You're in your living room. Who's going see?"

"Camden, I'm still struggling with my sexuality."

He leaned forward and mouthed the words "Who are you?"

I shrugged. "I'm not sure myself, anymore."

"You know that celebrity crowd and that guy you look like. The one named Tayler. He found a way out of the doldrums, didn't he? I mean, even if he looked homosexual, he hooked up with the goddess of the social set. Yet I could never work out why he didn't just become Connor's sidekick."

"Perhaps he's got some more experimenting to do?"

"What do you suppose he's making of the sham trial?"

"That the lunatics have taken over the asylum, and somehow that asylum's become as big as Astra City itself."

"What about beyond the city zone?"

"I've never ventured that far."

"But you've met people on SMC in other countries, haven't you?"

"I'm not sure. I question if they are from other countries."

"You know, one of my former online friends slipped out of his posh British accent from time to time. I never said anything, but it got me thinking. Do we ever really know the people we meet?"

"I want to know you, Camden."

"Ditto. It seems we share the same views. I want to meet you in person."

I looked at his file. A tear fell onto his image. "I want to meet you too."

"You don't need to tell me what's wrong. I think I know."

The computer went dead. I wiped my eyes and stared at the blank screen as time stood still. I forced my emotions aside, yet one by one, they struck me like violent intruders. And even with the dead screen, Camden's loving heart was reaching out from some forgotten corner of the city in an attempt to find mine, but my heart was out to sea. No one would touch it. Not Madi. Not Camden.

The intercom buzzed. " You can come out now." It was the steady voice of the Government. "It's time for feedback."

As I stepped outside my door, Number Thirteen pointed his shock ray at my chest.

"Tayler, you're discovering too many secrets." Stuart's stature was presidential.

Another door opened. A familiar figure wandered down the hall. He halted as soon as we recognized each other. More of this twisted jigsaw came to light.

It was Bernard, my landlady's former love interest. In the minutes that had just passed, he too had a message to convey. And if that message was not being listened to, then the incompliant individual on the receiving end of Social Media Central would be shoved toward a smaller group of contacts. Their world would shrink as it had for Mary. And as it had for Camden.

And even though I was beaten, a senseless will to survive was tapping me on the shoulder. As the Government turned to see who I was looking at, I made an assumption that Number Thirteen was doing the same. I took a chance, blindly elbowing him in the jaw before snatching the weapon out of his hand.

It did shoot, discharging a bolt that singed the wall. I aimed at the Government. Number Thirteen nursed his bloody mouth. As I backed toward the entrance, my trigger finger itched. Common sense told me the only way out was to shoot. I did. Stuart hit the floor, shrieking. His body quivered as he watched me run out the door.

Number Thirteen ran after me, but as I took aim, he blew a red-stained kiss before faking a scream and dropping to the ground. I quickly walked to the exit, still aiming at his porn-star body just in case. I hid the gun in my pocket and wandered outside. I passed the guards, bidding good night on my way out. They smiled back, letting me casually escape.

I was in dense bush before I heard their frantic footsteps in the distance. I stood nervously, waiting it out. In time, boots crunched through crumpled leaves with deadly intent, their erratic strides coming nearer and nearer. I froze, out in the open. There was no escape.

"Power Dude is getting out of hand," said a lone voice in the woods. He expelled breath between each syllable. His footsteps ceased.

"We have orders, mate" came the reply. "We have orders."

I didn't breathe and clutched onto a tree like I was locked to it. My feet didn't dare rustle the foliage.

"You said yourself, you're sick of him."

"Yeah, but we have a job to do."

"Do we?"

"You heard him. We have to find that guy that walked past us."

"You mean Tayler?"

"I thought it was him. That's the one with the hot chick."

"Yep, that's him. But what on earth could a guy like that do that's so evil?"

"His gal murdered someone."

"We don't know that."

"Anyway, it's illegal for us to give up the chase."

"But it's immoral for us to continue. You don't know what Power Dude wants with him. He's loony." The long silence that followed had me bathing in my own sweat. "Come on, let's head back slow. We'll say we couldn't find Tayler."

"I could report you for saying that."

"But I know you won't. You hate Power Dude's guts, too."

Another silence, and then their footsteps casually headed away. I still stayed quiet. An orchestra known as nature filled the void. Creatures whistled and grunted in the shadows. Tales were being shared by the forest folk.

I looked up. White specks greeted me from the faultless sky. The stars beamed down so sharply, I stood in awe. This was real. It wasn't a picture or a post. Their light had taken so long to reach me, I was seeing ghosts. Ghosts of civilizations forgotten. Ghosts of animals or vegetation never discovered. Ghosts of worlds unimaginable.

The forest was watching with me, calling out to our interplanetary neighbors both past and present. And here I was, with drama around me, yet insignificant in the grand scheme of things. I didn't bother to take a picture on my device. An image could never capture what was in my heart.

Eventually I walked, thinking calmly about things that would usually make me restless. I considered my landlady and her fate. She was off to see charlatans in foreign lands who existed inside the compound I had left. *Where will she end up?*

Tranquility turned to concern as Camden's thoughtful face haunted me. Did he pull the plug on our conversation once he knew the truth, or did the authorities kill his feed? I wanted to see him. He was a kindred spirit. *But is that the only reason I yearn to meet him?* No. He was my flirtatious rebound after finding the truth about Madi. *But why am I drawn to a man?* My head ached of uncertainty, so I looked back to the sky.

The stars were fading, slipping away to let dawn break. Birds sang their tune to welcome the new canvas above. Orange was its first coat. Blue waited on the edge. Calm floated down in the mist.

As I took another step, I realized I couldn't go home. So I headed for the only destination I could think of.

# Nineteen

"TAYLER, YOUR FACE disturbs me," said Felicity. She left the closed sign up, then ushered me to the back of her store.

"What's wrong with my face?"

"It's the face of a madman."

I rubbed my cheeks. "Really?" I could hear my voice deflate.

"Did anyone see you come in?"

"A couple with a baby carriage nearly looked back when they left your shop. I must have been running too loudly. Fortunately, their baby mumbled something and they got all coy. If either of them caught a glimpse of me, they didn't turn back to verify who I was."

"How long were you waiting outside?"

"Too long."

"Did you see Connor and Madeline?"

I paused. I was still dealing with everything I'd experienced. My brain turned to toffee, stretching and rearranging the facts over and over. Yet I owed Felicity some kind of answer.

"Connor's locked up. Madeline, well, let me tell you about her later. It will explain my madman face."

"Are they safe?"

"I think so. Actually, I don't know."

"What do you mean?"

"I'll sound even more like a madman if I tell you."

"You need to get your thoughts together." She opened the lone door on the far wall and pushed me through. "Shower, just to the right. Towels are in that cupboard, there. I'll bring in some of Shaun's clothes."

"How is Shaun? Where is he?"

"I can't tell you, but he's safe."

"How safe are you?"

"So far, so good. No one has approached me about any of this. Now jump in the shower. I'll return with a pair of his jeans and a shirt for you and leave them on the table next to the door." She promptly shut the door.

I welcomed the warm stream. My aching joints revitalized with each drop as if vital minerals were being added to my body by some mystic force. And as I came to life, the stench of fear washed away down the plughole.

"Just roll up the jeans and they should fit," Felicity called. "And check the pocket when you get dressed." Again, the door shut.

I dried off as an image of Camden flashed before me, arousing me. I gripped myself, but this was neither the time nor the place. My grubby jeans and that T-shirt lay on the cold tiles. And in that pile, something stood as stiff as me. I rummaged, finding the gun I had escaped with.

I laid it on the table as I slipped Shaun's jeans on. I buttoned the shirt, and as I reached for the stolen weapon, I remembered to check my pocket. Inside was a note with handwritten directions. I kept it in my palm and slid the gun as far down the front of the jeans as I could, leaving my shirt untucked to hide the bulges. I reentered the shop and browsed one of the five bookcases, finally taking a volume from its shelf.

The other customer in the store was about forty years of age and sweated glamour through every pore of her body.

Her ginger hair matched her fur coat, as if she'd found dye to complement the color of her strands. She clutched a quaint fawn handbag close to her body, keeping it safe from imaginary thieves. But then her device rang with the sound of wind-chimes. She pulled it out, dazzling me with the number of diamonds sewn onto its protective case.

"That's an excellent book," Felicity said. She strode my way, giving me a stern look. "I recommend it. Great writer."

Her own device was in her hand, but as she passed it over mine, it made no sound. It was turned off. This was a fake transaction. There'd be no record of me being in her shop. And besides, I doubted I had access to funds, anyway.

"Thank you," I replied.

I went outside, took a deep breath, and searched for an empty street. The directions were moist in my clammy palm, but none of the ink had run. I was supposed to turn left after leaving the shop but was now in the opposite direction. I wandered back on the right path, checking the store from across the road.

Felicity was clever enough not to include any street names on the instructions, just landmarks. The egg-splattered Keep Left sign. The hobo shelter made of old wooden planks and plastic bags. The garbage cans surrounded by a pile of rubbish, which no sanitation workers could drive close enough to with their trucks. For some unknown reason, I tossed the book into the heap.

I headed toward Breaker Street where the ghostly inhabitants hid behind closed curtains. Frazer Road was the same, as was Celeste Court, citizens recklessly sharing their points of view with departmental strangers analyzing every word. Eventually, I came to the second building with a glass door on the street I believed was the right one. I pressed the buzzer for apartment eight.

"Come in." It was Mike's voice, the author whose book launch we attended. "Head straight upstairs."

His welcoming smile was accompanied by a nervous twitch. He grabbed me and hauled me inside. His place was a bedsit. An oversized couch filled half the room, facing several plush armchairs. An oversized suitcase acted as a coffee table. On top sat a rainbow-colored bong and a small tin of weed.

His bed was a basic double futon with little charm. But next to it was an ancient television, a relic from the early days of streamed entertainment when images were portrayed in monochrome. Scratchy gold material hid its speaker and a huge metal knob sat above several smaller ones, like a row of buttons on a shirt. Thankfully, this was the only screen visible.

"I wasn't sure who Felicity would send me to, but I'm glad it's you."

"I feel like you're going to attack me."

"What?"

"Your eyes look like they've been touched by pure evil."

"Felicity said something similar. She said I had the face of a madman."

"Sit down and have a smoke." He opened the small overhead fridge above the sink and pulled out a bottle of vodka and a couple of limes. "I don't have soda. Will water do?" He sounded timid.

"At this point, I don't care what I drink. Just pour it and sit down. I have a tale you won't believe."

I eyed the bong, knowing it was a bad idea. I was a marked man. I had to stay focused. But who was I kidding? I was about to drink vodka. I snatched the bong and shoved the instrument of sedation to my lips. Before long, the hazy essence filled my lungs. I breathed out its magic pattern. I slumped deep into the lush cushion behind me.

"Here, drink this."

I gulped it down in one hit.

"More?"

I shook my head. "I'm easing."

"You're easing?"

I raised my palm, bobbing it like a yacht on calm water. "You know, easing."

"Is this the wrong time to ask about Madeline Q and Connor?"

"Oh dear. Madi!"

"What happened?"

"Crazy stuff. I'm definitely single again."

I crammed more weed into the burnished cone and lit it. I sucked in the smoldering intruder, slammed down the bong, and clutched Mike on both cheeks. His lips parted as I pulled him near; my tainted smoke darted down his throat. He blew it back on my face, reached for the back of my neck, and planted his gentle kiss.

One led to another. Small pecks of tenderness, each telling me something different. He raised me from the sofa, slid his body down, and reached for my fly. I stopped him and undid my jeans myself, carefully making sure the gun didn't slip out as I slid my pants to the floor.

He glided his thumb over the wet patch on my briefs. My stiffness bulged against the cotton as he moistened the fabric even more with his circling fingertip. His tongue tasted the damp. He reached inside and pulled out my eager friend.

We made love while I took more hits from the bong to quiet my inner demons. I rode him, and for some lightheaded reason, I let him ride me. And it wasn't weird or dirty. It was hot and steamy and loving in the way I'd experienced with women.

I sat and cried on his futon. He cradled me. I finally whimpered before sighing in relief.

"That was your first time with a man, wasn't it?"

"I've perved. I've kissed one. Well, I've kissed two now. But yes, that was my first time with a man. And I'm glad it was with you."

His sheepish grin made me want to melt into him, but as I glanced at Shaun's rolled-up jeans on the knotted floorboards, fear rendered me speechless.

"You're well and truly haunted, aren't you?"

I looked to the ceiling with teary eyes.

"Talk about it." He packed another cone, lit it, and shoved it squarely in my face. "You have to talk about it."

I smoked. Its mischievous medicine loosened the grip on my tongue. "Where's Shaun?"

"Felicity told me not to tell you. Just for his own safety."

"Can you give me a hint?"

"He's gone to stay with someone he met."

"One of his conquests?"

"No. Someone from out of town. A fan who admired him on his Lover Net blog."

"You're kidding?"

"No. They met in person before Shaun was taken to his place."

"No!" I stood. "No! He's a dead man."

"He's perfectly okay. Felicity went with him to meet the guy he's staying with."

"You can't trust anyone, Mike. Do you hear me? You can't trust anyone on the internet."

"What are you going on about?"

"They're all liars. Every one of them. There's a big room where people pretend to be friends and followers and caring individuals, but they're planted by the Government."

"What are you getting at?"

I jumped onto the couch, frantically acting out my words. "There's a secret compound. Room upon room upon room. Each one is a private individual world where people fake being friends with people in the real world. They get them to shrink their circle, making lines of communication narrower and narrower. Everyone is being trained in what they should think and say, and if they don't comply, new people enter their world to try to tame them."

"Huh?" He got dressed and encouraged me to do the same. I slid on my underwear. "Hey, I know the Government paid you guys to keep their message on track. It was dishonest, but spin-doctoring has been around since god knows when, so I can overlook it. I even get the Government turning against you because you went off message." He stood and began to pace. "A room, you say?"

"Many rooms, decked out like people's homes. I saw Bernard."

"Bernard who?"

"One of the men my landlady flirted with before he was dismissed so her world would become smaller. Last I knew, she only spoke to two other individuals. And now I know they're fake."

Mike stopped pacing and poured more vodka. "If some people are fake, then it stands to reason that others have to be real."

"Until they separate you from the real ones."

"This is mad."

"So you believe me?" I asked.

"How do you know all this?"

"I was there. That's where I ended up after going to the police station."

"Our city is more corrupt than I gave it credit for." He placed the drink in front of me before taking his seat. "That sounds mind-boggling, and yet with everything the Government has done, it's believable. Kind of. Maybe. Hmm." He sipped. "Now tell me, how are Madeline Q and Connor?"

I shivered, then raised myself.

"Are you leaving?"

"We had sex."

"Yeah."

"Madi and I had sex."

"Right."

"So, who are you?"

"You know who I am. I'm Mike."

"Who are you really?"

"What's going on, Tayler?"

"That's what I want to know."

"Calm down. I'm Mike, the guy you made love with."

"But there's a pattern here. A pattern I have to break. No one is who they say they are. Everyone has a motive."

"Is that you talking or the dope?"

"Oh it's me, and I can see clearly. How do I know that you're not more than just a writer?"

He stood. I sprung backward. He stepped toward me, so I bolted from his apartment, barefoot and underdressed.

# Twenty

I STOOD IN the park, pissing against a tree. Onlookers stared, took photographs, and uploaded. I had their attention. Now it was time for their savior in underwear to tell them the truth.

I tucked my penis away and extended my arms in a grand gesture above my head. Theatrics would be the key to my success.

"You're Tayler, aren't you?" asked a frizzy-haired girl.

"I'm many things, sweetheart. Bi. Vocal. Devious. Maybe even deranged. But today, I'm your preacher."

I saw the record light go on from her device. Others also began to video me, but one bearded man stepped forward, eyed me from head to toe, and listened without recording.

"Small people. Yes, you're the small people. Cows. Sheep. People. The herd, that's what you are. The herd." The midday sun was glaring. I needed sleep. "Who here voted for the Government?"

"People are supposed to vote him in?" said the girl.

"Hell, I bet you don't even know what he looks like. I sure as hell didn't when I met him."

"I don't believe the polls are real," the bearded one stated.

"I don't either," I declared. "I thought, maybe, some of you voted for Stuart. Oops. That's right. We're supposed to use his august title while he's in office. But you may be right. Perhaps he's just in power because he just is. When was the last confounded election?"

"Three years ago," said a woman with a dog on a leash. The collar had a small light next to a lens.

"No, it was last year," said the man with facial hair.

"What's your name, sir?" I had to know.

"Kinsey."

"So, Kinsey, you voted. Who else did? Go on, hands up." Only one other raised their hand. "See, we don't even know when we're supposed to vote. Yet surely my ex-girlfriend and the other social media celebrities would have slipped it in and reminded you. But I guess Stuart didn't want you to know. He didn't want to give up power. And maybe it didn't matter. Maybe it was all rigged, anyway."

A few murmured. A few giggled.

"Shh," said Kinsey. His finger landed on his lips.

"Oh, let them laugh. They won't be laughing when they hear my tale." I turned to the girl. "Are you recording this? Have you got my best side?"

"I'm streaming you live."

"Good for you. That's just what I need. Anyone watching?"

"It's trending."

"I'm streaming too," called a tattooed biker girl in the back. "Hashtag Tayler. You've been out of the spotlight for a few days. People are commenting."

"Great," I said. "Let's broadcast the truth." I wandered to the bench where I'd first met Stuart, and the others followed like paparazzi. "This is where it started. I met the man in power, and I didn't recognize him. How many of you actually know who the Government is at the moment?"

"Stuart Manning," Kinsey said. "He was the CEO of Social Media Central before he became our leader."

"You know more than me, it seems. Most of you don't even know who's in power or actually care. As long as you can mirror meal or flirt or upload shit, you don't care."

"Or we do Movie Nights," called the woman with the dog. "We have to thank you guys for that trend."

"Well, hold on to that. Stay connected, but do it with people you knew before you hooked into Social Media Central. In fact, just meet face to face with the members of your family or the people in your office, if you haven't been forced to work online. Because just about everyone you meet solely on Social Media Central is fake."

More murmurs, but this time, they sounded sarcastic.

"What do you mean by fake?" Kinsey asked.

"They're psychiatrists, I think, acting like ordinary people." Now even my ardent follower raised a brow. "No, hear me out. Who here has followed the sham court case against Madeline Q and Connor?"

"Me," the dog owner said. A few others raised their hands, including a group who had just arrived.

"Have any of you voted?"

"I tried to vote *innocent,* but I don't think my vote was counted," Kinsey replied.

"Why do you say that?"

"The graph didn't go up on the *innocent* side, but the *guilty* verdict kept rising."

"Were you surprised?"

"Not really."

"What has this to do with us?" the wiry-haired girl asked.

"It has *everything* to do with you," I barked.

In the distance even more came to join my media event, including Mike and Felicity. The author and the bookseller wandered through the audience like thieves trying not to wake the family pet. As for the girl, she stopped streaming me, shrugged, and walked away. But several devices were still pointed in my direction. I sat on the bench, forgetting there was only one piece of fabric between me and the planks of wood. A splinter scraped my ass, but I didn't wince like a coward. Hey, I was on camera.

"What has it to do with us, Tayler?" The dog owner repeated the girl's question.

"There's a secret compound in the forest where your fake social-media friends talk to you from their makeshift rooms made up to look like actual homes."

Many grimaced.

"And they're herding you into smaller and smaller circles so they can reach you one on one."

"Why are they doing that?" Felicity asked.

"Everyone, you need to meet my friends. This is Felicity. So sweet she farts talcum powder. And this is Mike. He's a horny lad. He'll get you at a weak moment."

"So, why did they kill Candy?" Mike asked.

"They needed a body. Isn't it obvious, lover boy? We stepped outside our circle and became too big for our boots. They had to kill someone. Why not a small-town girl?" I pointed. "You. And you. All of you. You've all been given a little drama to make you wary of us. Disclaim us as if we were never worth knowing about."

"But you are. Or were." This outburst came from the biker woman.

"Until we expanded your horizons in the other direction, counteracting the smaller and smaller worlds you inhabit. So, Stuart—sorry, the Government—fought back. But he still has fake people designated to act like your SMC friends and guide you away from any sliver of reality. You're battery hens. Connor knew this. That's why he's locked up!"

"He confessed to a murder. That's why he's locked up." The tattooed biker also stopped streaming me. "You're a goose, mate. Dead girl, sharp knife, guilty confessions. Hey, who needs to vote on their trial? We know the outcome."

"Yes, ask yourselves that. Why vote if there's a confession? No motive. But there's a confession or two, which, in an age where everything is videoed, no one has ever seen."

There was a murmur.

"I thought so. Most of you didn't care enough to look for the video. It would be too long to watch. Instead, everything is hearsay. You just read it on a post and share the news, without the facts. You spineless idiots!"

"I think it's time to go home, Tayler." Mike seemed sincere, but I wasn't buying it.

"I haven't got to the good part yet. I saw the rooms. The fake ones where people are employed to be your friends. I had to pretend to convince some guy called Camden to join some new part of Social Media Central."

"You were one of the fakes?" the biker asked.

"Yes. I was mistaken for one of their cronies."

"Tayler, everyone knows who you are. You wouldn't have been mistaken for anyone."

"Believe it or not, the supervisor had no idea who I was."

"You're full of horse manure, mate. Your friends are guilty, and you're making up stories."

"Yeah. That photo proves it," yelled the girl.

"What photo?"

"That famous selfie of the dead girl with you, Connor, and your girlfriend."

"What? The one where we're smiling with Candy?"

"No," said the bikie. "The one where Madeline Q is obviously jealous of your attachment to the dead girl. It's got you and Connor in it, but it's not on any profile. It's part of the evidence."

"Are you hearing yourselves?" I screamed.

An unearthly rumble echoed from the buildings. Kinsey asked if I knew what was going on. Mike and Felicity looked at each other as if fragments of the sky were falling. The rumble repeated itself, harsher. A few citizens hit the ground as if there was an air raid. We waited.

Thoughts of space saucers entered my mind. They'd land and their captain would signal me through telepathy. He'd know we need their help. His army and I would storm Stuart's compound and evaporate all the fakes. Madi would be captured, tied up, and sent back to me.

Another rumble, this time, quieter. More bewildered folk flooded the park as if an earthquake was about to hit.

The sound of screeching tires came from the tattooed woman's screen, which was still nestled in her palm. Soon after, various other notification sounds demanded attention. Even Felicity and Mike checked their screens. Now the ever-increasing horde read in silence.

"What does it say?"

"This is the Government," Kinsey quoted. "Please don't be alarmed. We are investigating the disturbance and will keep you informed as soon as we know the cause."

"More smoke and mirrors."

"What are you talking about?" asked one of the newcomers. Her dyed-black hair couldn't hide her age.

"The Government is still pulling the strings. You think this wasn't planned? A spooky noise reverberating through the city to make you all take notice."

"But you said we were being siphoned off into smaller and smaller circles." The dog owner threw my words back in my face.

"Yeah!" added the biker girl. "If this is something the Government has set up, then it will bring us together."

"Isn't it obvious? It's their new plan." Felicity and Mike joined me on the bench. "Think about it. When have they ever reached out *en masse* like this before? Never. Their plan failed when we suggested Movie Night. You all went out and met people face to face. So why not fight fire with fire? Control the conversation. Get you panicked so Stuart can send you little alerts to zombify you into submission."

"But there was a freaky noise," said Felicity. "And it was uber loud that first time. Maybe this is for real?"

"Rubbish!"

Some of the audience chattered while many of the newer visitors to the park began to stroll away.

Biker girl stepped forward and stared me right in the face. "One minute, it's fake people to keep us apart; the next, it's getting us talking with each other over a strange sound. Do you know where you stand, Tayler?"

"Yes, I do! Now you'll be using your devices again, searching for information on what just happened. You'll be hooked on Social Media Central before you realize you actually can't live without it. And when you realize it was some grand plan, you'll still be hooked to your screens telling each other how stupid you all were."

"And then we'll blame the Government. Your argument is flawed."

"It might not be," said Kinsey.

"Go home with your friends, Tayler."

More of my audience were leaving.

"We should follow their lead," said Mike.

I glanced at Kinsey. He pouted as I considered borrowing that lady's dog collar and walking him home. *When did I get so kinky?* I ran my hands through my scruffy hair. Mike snapped his fingers in front of my face before glaring down his nose at me. Soon, he and Felicity grabbed me, pulled me off the bench, and guided me through a city of mystified citizens.

# Twenty-One

"YOU WANTED TO sleep with that Kinsey dude," Mike alleged.

"What? Me? No. Get real! He's cute. Very cute. But sex. Nah."

Felicity and Mike took me back to his studio apartment. They got me to talk about the fake social-media friends and the Government's secret compound. Personally, I didn't think they believed me.

In the middle of my interrogation, Felicity got a call from Shaun. He was back in Astra City and waiting outside her apartment block. She raced out, hardly saying goodbye.

"Tayler, you haven't answered me. With everything you've seen, why were you going to trust Kinsey, a stranger?"

"Why do we trust anyone, Mike? Because we have to."

"You want to have sex with him."

"Do I sniff jealousy?"

"Just because we had sex, doesn't make us a couple."

"Then you have no right to question me."

I was sinking into one of the oversized couches. Sleep was encroaching like a disease. Mike got up to make me a cup of coffee.

Through blurred eyes, I glanced at the pile of books on the suitcase acting as a coffee table. On top was Mike's novel with a lonely face on the cover. Even though I'd seen it before, it called to my waning senses.

"Is it true that authors write about their own experiences?" I asked.

"With a heavy dose of fiction piled on top."

"The cover reminds me of you."

"Do you know me well enough to make that assumption?"

"But people's faces, they have history. The drawn character on the sleeve seems like the type of person who's been hurt by love. Unsure of who to trust. Scared to make the same mistakes."

"You can tell all that from the cover?" His voice was deadpan.

"I think everyone at our age has felt that."

Mike placed our beverages down and lowered himself into the larger of two armchairs.

"The milk in my coffee is really frothy. Where did you learn to do that?"

"Have you ever heard of a rich author? No, I thought not. There's a new coffee shop in a posh neighborhood where I've learned to barista."

I sipped. The brew warmed my palate as I groaned as if I was on heat.

"You're just moaning because you're tired."

"Mike."

"Yes."

"I think we have more in common than I realized."

"You didn't think that when you ran out my door in your underwear."

I studied my brew, not quite knowing if my cheeks felt warm through its heat or my shame.

"Can I ask you something?"

"Of course."

"Do you remember school?"

"When I was very young."

"What do you remember?"

"Friends. Friends that I could play with and touch. Friends that I knew not only from sight, but from their smell, their facial expressions, and the tone of their voice."

"But surely you had friends later in life. Felicity's a friend."

"One of the few I know personally. Why are you asking me this?"

"As a teenager, I really wanted that sense of camaraderie I had when I was young, even though most of that time is now a faded memory. But I remember the sensation. That sensation of teaming up with two other friends and sitting at a tea party with an evil queen and a superhero-in-training. Oh, don't look at me like that. I know I'm blabbering."

"Go on. I think I'm on your page."

"Of course there was no evil queen or hero, just two of my friends playing imaginary roles while we sat on kid-sized chairs at a table. But that's the way we'd eat our lunch. We'd imagine we were sorcerers gaining magic through each bite, or spiders with insect sandwiches to munch. Sometimes more friends would join in, making it more fun. And that's what I miss. As more would join us, there'd be other personalities to explore. The confident kid who barged in on any game. The quiet ones who I always felt comfortable near. The bossy ones who someone would eventually stand up to. And that's what I wanted as a teenager. A group of friends to have adventures with. To argue with. To help if I could, or to help me when I needed to talk about the difficult things."

"Yeah, I hear what you're saying. Those teen years were hard when all you have is online chat. When I was at school for a brief few years, I had a friend that was also named Mike. To avoid confusion, our teacher would call me Michael and him, Mike. I knew he didn't like lettuce. I knew he never liked to walk on the cracks of the pavement. Hell, I even knew what his farts sounded like."

"What did he know about you?"

"He knew I'd eat the lettuce from his sandwiches. He knew mosquitoes liked to bite me on the ankles. And he knew what my frown looked like, and always asked if I was feeling all right. And yes, I too miss that sensation. That sensation of people being jigsaw pieces that fit in different ways for different people. That emotional mass that interweaved in the classroom like a delicately balanced ecosystem, and when a new kid arrived, time would be taken to squeeze them in and realign the balance. And each of us knew when it was our time to shine, or when it was important for someone else to."

"Rather than all of us trying to get a look in on Social Media Central."

"Tayler, you don't have an online profile."

"I'm online by association, and as soon as the telephony system is laid to rest, I too will be forced to have an SMC profile."

"Regardless, that's why I like you. As someone once said to me, how much of a narcissist do you have to be to star on Social Media Central?"

"Are you saying I'm a narcissist?"

"I guess I just did. I didn't make my point very clear."

"Don't worry, I know what you meant. The geeks invented the ultimate popularity contest when social media was born. I like to think I'm the least narcissistic of that group, but I have been seduced a little more than I'd like to admit."

"You're not as bad as some of the others."

"What, like Connor or Shaun?"

"Connor's the least narcissistic. He's an artist."

"But Madeline Q is the most narcissistic. There! I said it. Surprised?" I couldn't stop a grin spreading across my cheeks.

"Tayler, you're shaking."

He was right. My coffee was in danger of spilling on his couch. He took the cup with both hands and set it down.

"You know, Mike, I have the family photos on the thumb drive attached to my keys. I have another copy of the folder on another thumb drive in the apartment I can't go back to. That is, if any of my possessions are still there." I took out my mobile device. "But here in my window to the world, I haven't copied those pictures."

"I'm listening. Go on."

"I don't look at those pictures much, although I did recently. When I looked for too long, I got sad. There's not one image of me alone. There's my mum and dad, or all three of us, but I'm always in the background. They're never looking at what I'm doing. Their faces are staring straight at the lens as if everyone cared who they were."

"I have a feeling you never look at their online feeds."

"I know what I'll see. They never surprise me."

"Not even to see what they're saying about their famous son?"

"I don't care."

"So what's this got to do with Ms. Madeline Q?"

I picked up my cup, took a sip, but my hand started shaking again. He took it by the handle and placed it back down.

"You know, she's not in any danger. She never was. She's a pawn of the Government." I paused.

"Tayler, I'm listening."

"She was the real evil queen, not like the one my childhood friends would act out at lunchtime. She courted me for heaven knows what reason. Yet she knew the Government intimately."

"Are you sure?"

"She had sex with him right before my eyes. I shocked you, Mike. Aren't I a clever lad? When this whole affair started, I was too scared to share my opinions, but thanks to Madeline Q, I am now just putting it all out there, warts and all."

"You've startled me more than shocked me, but you need to get this off your chest."

"From the very start, she was waiting. In fact, they both were. Two deceitful game players looking for a pawn. And I showed up. The ruler and the tart looking for a victim or a stereotype or something."

"You're not a stereotype."

"Yes, I am. You see, I was the forgotten audience, and hell, they got that so right. I wasn't the desperate older woman flirting with every available man online. I wasn't the skilled photographer capturing glamorous nobodies for blog posts no one remembers the next day. I wasn't the seasoned lover who could tantalize my readers, while at the same time awakening a sense of connection. No. I was the freak that no one listened to."

"And how exactly was Madi part of this?"

"She pulled me into her web of lies and deceit just to make me a somebody for someone else's marketing needs."

"My friend, are Madi and Connor safe?"

"Madi, for sure. She was never in danger. She knows Stuart. They were grinding long before I came onto the scene. And Connor. He's probably okay. After all, he was Madeline Q's bosom buddy years before I stumbled into her trap."

He passed me a handkerchief from his jean pocket. "It's clean. Take it."

"I'm not going to cry."

"Trust me, you're about to."

"I'm too tired to cry."

I choked on that last word. Soon I was blubbering. As her face haunted my thoughts, I howled. When the sickening image of her riding Stuart Manning slammed into my skull, I bashed my fist on the armrest. And as her body came to mind lying peacefully in her own bed, I wondered where the hell I'd gone wrong.

# Twenty-Two

"No, no. Don't use my real name," I said. "Everyone knows me."

"What do you want to be known as?" Mike asked.

"What's the most boring name you can think of?"

"Tim."

"No. Tim is a person who's cute and knows how to use his bedroom eyes."

"Peter."

"Peter has personality and charm, and can be a larrikin from time to time."

"Paul?"

"No. John."

"You don't look like a John."

"That's the point."

"Come to think of it, you don't look like a Tim or Peter or a Paul."

"But John's the most boring."

He typed in my new identity, 'John24' and handed my device back to me. "Pick a password."

I entered one on a curious site that had nothing to do with Social Media Central. Like a spy on a mission, Mike arranged for a friend of his to call in earlier that day.

"I like the metallic blue case on your device," said the mystery man. He was inspecting it closely. "They're making some fantastic shades these days." His vintage doctor's bag was oddly the same hue.

"It's called Midnight Blue," I said.

"There's nothing 'midnight' about it," Mike noted. "Marketers are getting more and more uninspired."

"I didn't catch your name." I leaned forward.

"No names," the man insisted. "I don't need to know you, and you don't need to know me." He broke out in a twisted smile, that smirk of recognition I now knew too well.

He pulled out a screwdriver and proceeded to open my screen. Inside his bag were thirty or so microchips all the same color, and all protected in clear plastic sleeves. They were held securely to the inside walls away from the tools, which were at the bottom.

With steady fingers, he fished out one of the many chips from my device. He carefully scrutinized one of his own chips against the soft light filtering through the lone window before inserting it into the machine. He screwed the back shield on tight and laid the device in his palm, handing it to me like it was a sacred object.

"My work here is done," he said.

"Do I owe you anything for whatever it is you've just done?"

"Your open mind is reward enough for me."

Mike let him out while thanking him wholeheartedly. I turned on my screen and stared at the Social Media Central logo, which always made its presence felt when anyone's device was warming up.

"Press your volume button and your on-off switch simultaneously," Mike commanded.

"Do I turn the volume up or down?"

"It doesn't matter."

I did. Another logo appeared. In simple red lettering, the words *Alta Net* filled the screen. Soon a simple homepage greeted me with various blog posts. I studied the site, flicking through topics as diverse as *A new government—it's time for rebellion* to an odd one titled, *Did Goth exist?*

"What am I looking at?"

"A secret site for the openminded."

"And this has nothing to do with Social Media Central?"

"No, it doesn't. It's the Alta Net."

"The what?"

"The Alternative Net, or Alta Net for short. It's for people like you and me. Those that can see the shades of gray between the shades of gray."

That's when Mike took my device and set up my profile. Then he found his own profile and connected us.

"Michael3? Why not Mike3?"

"My parents call me Michael. It just sounds nicer."

Soon after, my addiction began. At first I just read. I read articles on the historical decline of leaders who brought their people together, rather than dividing them. I read about the history of the moving image and, as I often did, longed to laugh with a group of people in a cinema. I found out what those printed things were that spun around toward the screen in the older movies I usually watched. And I eventually took in videos of early vlogs of teenagers talking about their lives, even though the resolution of these was hard on the eyes.

One fascinated me in particular. It was shot near a river with several teens singing along with a friend who was strumming his guitar. They looked so connected. One girl leaned into her boyfriend, both wearing contented smiles and oversized pullovers.

They all knew the words of the song. *How can they all know the words to the same song?* I decided that they must have practiced for this video, even though it felt as if they were being spontaneous.

And then there was this clip of a kid who threw this round thing forward, but it was attached to a string. And he moved his hands all over the place, and the string and this rotating thing followed, wrapping itself around his arms yet never losing its momentum. The video was called *Yoyo. Is that the kid's name? And what is that thing he's playing with?* I often went back to watch it.

In another section of the Alta Net, someone had meticulously typed out the diary of her great-great-grandmother, which she posted in chapters every couple of days. I was hooked. I couldn't believe friends and neighbors used to call in without making an appointment. How rude. Tea and biscuits even had to be bought in preparation for these impromptu intruders.

Several entries talked of long phone conversations. Seriously, her generation had too much time on their hands.

Then there were the discussions. Some had tried the "house party" option with the Life Experience Mob. In a warehouse somewhere, an old-fashioned street had been built. A few old cars were created and parked in front of homes. Some people complained because they couldn't go inside the homes, but most didn't mind. They could still peer through a window where a forgotten world of fireplaces and televisions were set up.

And the folk chatting about it on the Alta Net got dressed up as families or as couples. One woman had a selfie of herself in pigtails while she chewed something called gum. They shared food that was laid out on blankets spread out on lawns. They had to string shiny weird metallic snakes on the houses. Apparently, it was once a December tradition.

I asked if anyone knew if this company recreated a school. Some said it was in the works and immediately began the discussion on how bad, or good, the education was of those of my generation. And people suddenly connected with me. Well, they were John24's connections, not Tayler's. And to keep my anonymity, I found a photo of a toy truck to replace my absent profile picture.

Several days after being seduced into this electronic world, I read about Goth Industries. I compared debate between the Alta Net and Social Media Central. SMC reported that an old unused uranium mine not far outside Astra City was leaking radiation. As yet, no one had been affected. But the Government was weighing into discussions, letting people know that a team of experts were on the case. I wondered what type of experts had been sent. Apparently, the weird rumble heard around our city had something to do with the unsteady mine, courtesy of Goth Industries.

Over on the alternative site, everyone was debating the likelihood of an old mine causing small tremors. Even more curious was the fact that no one recalled ever hearing of this Indian-based company. And though I knew little about industry, I was just as cynical in my comments.

Twenty-four hours later, SMC launched *The Way We Were*. Its first article reprinted snippets from *Gazettes* and *Heralds* about India. I read, surprised to learn that this little country led the free world in the past century, whatever a "free world" was supposed to be.

And the following day, another snippet was published, this time from a *Chronicle* of the late 1900s. India's astronauts were the first in space. *Go figure?*

But in the afternoon, small snippets of video were being shared of sick people in beds. One face haunted me in particular. His face as gray as concrete. His eyes bulging like a fly's. His mouth always open as if trying to vomit.

I slapped myself in the face. Fake people, now fake videos. *What was I thinking?* I switched to the Alta Net and publicly questioned the validity of the leaked footage.

The day after, I had twelve new connections. Instantly, I connected back. When I asked why the Government was trying to make us believe there was a radiation leak, fifty-seven more people decided to connect with me. And when I came up with the theory that some friends on Social Media Central were cleverly planted fakes, my connection counter shot up to two hundred and thirty-nine.

And then I remembered something I should've checked long before now. Candy's profile. Just as I feared, the selfie we took with her wasn't there. I suspected deletion.

I searched for the photo elsewhere on SMC and found it quickly, full of comments claiming Madeline Q looked protective of me and how dare this floozy come into our inner circle.

I looked a little closer at the screen, noting no hint of jealousy on Madi's face, even though it's what the bikie chick in the park claimed. I looked at the screen closer and saw the date stamp on the image had been tampered with for some reason. It showed a date six months prior.

If anyone had bothered to think about it, they would have worked out that I hadn't even met Connor or Madi that long ago, let alone the deceased. But who really paid attention to anything? I surprised myself at how I didn't dwell on any of this.

And at this time, I was a nomad. It was just me, my screen, Mike's pad, Felicity's place, and Shaun's new hangout.

After several weeks, I thought I found Kinsey, the bearded dude that was in the park the day of my notorious appearance in underwear. He'd posted an article about the most important of the Social Media Socialites, Tayler. He went on to talk about my accusation of actors posing as friends online. He said he was there the day I'd spoken freely.

I contacted him, wanting to know if he could join us at a gathering Felicity, Mike, and I were planning. He replied that he didn't live in Astra City and couldn't get time off work. It turned out he had found a job as a cook.

At times, I thought about Camden, the lonely guy I had to webcam at the Government's secret base. I blatantly asked if anyone knew him, but the answer was always the same.

"You should have reached out to him," Shaun said.

"I did. He worked out who I was, and shortly after, the screen went blank."

We were seated downstairs at the bookstore, waiting patiently.

"Do you think anyone else is coming?" Felicity asked. "It's getting dark."

"I promoted it to my connections. Someone should have turned up."

"How many responses did John24 get?" Mike asked.

"About eight of them sounded keen."

"Don't despair, Tayler. Those of us on the Alta Net stay anonymous. That's why we're not plugged into the official social media site."

"Is Tayler safe?"

"Safer than he'd be on Social Media Central."

Shaun nodded graciously. "Personally, I'm glad we're not entertaining strangers." He looked to Felicity who tried to smile.

"Strangers?" I queried half-jokingly. "Remember when they were followers or friends? Or even lovers in your case? And yes, you're right, Shaun, I don't know my connections personally, but I yearn to meet at least one of them. They're my kind."

He contemplated the floor.

"I think you should stop being John24 for the moment, and just be yourself," said Mike.

"What do you mean?"

"Have you asked Shaun about the follower he stayed with when the shit hit the fan?"

"Of course I did, but I got the feeling he didn't want to talk about it, did you, Shaun?"

"That's because I'm still getting my head around it."

"Who was he?" Mike asked. "For some reason, I got the notion that it was only women who used to follow your blog."

At this point, Felicity decided to put on a pot of tea.

"He was a guy I used to give tips to about lovemaking. He seemed like one of those older virgins but assured me he wasn't. So we'd speak online face to face, and I'd give him advice on how to ask the girl he liked out on a date. But he didn't even have the confidence to mirror meal, so he was still a work in progress."

"Not a bad cover," I said. "A guy, rather than one of your conquests, to hide out with."

"That was my idea," Felicity said. She lifted the kettle and poured the steaming water into the teapot.

"Only he wasn't what he seemed online," Shaun continued. "Even the bedroom where his computer was, was different to the one I saw in the background when we spoke."

I nodded knowingly.

"When I questioned him about it, he said he moved. And yes, that kind of makes sense, because he always claimed that he lived outside Astra City. But here we were, just uptown yet all that time we spent online he never mentioned wanting to move."

"How much did you share with him?"

"I decided not to mention Felicity. So I talked about my past lovers and what each one meant to me, but he occasionally turned the conversation into something dirty. The kind of dirty out of character from a guy with bugger-all experience."

"Did he ask about Madeline Q or Connor or me?"

"He did ask about you, Tayler, and I was honest. I said I didn't know where you were."

"Why did you decide to come back?" Mike asked.

One by one, Felicity passed us each a cup of raspberry tea, then sat next to her man with her own drink in hand.

"I got suspicious when I met this girl he knew. He was really comfortable with her. My gut instinct went into overdrive. I knew I'd be safer back here, so I left when he was asleep."

"Why did you wait until now to tell us?" I asked. "I mean, I told you all about the secret compound and the fake social-media friends. Why didn't you tell me then?"

He gritted his teeth and looked to Felicity. "Because it all seemed far-fetched."

"But you just said your gut instinct went into overdrive with that fan you stayed with. How could you not believe me?"

"I just needed time to take it in. Seriously, Madeline and her secret collaborator? A compound full of fake rooms with psychologists or actors taking us all for a ride? The very god I believed in, Social Media Central, being a tool of the Government?"

"But you knew that, Shaun. He paid us. Plus, you didn't treat SMC like a god you believed in. You treated the fans like we all did. Losers who needed a life."

"Yes, I know, but when I went into hiding, I realized SMC was the only identity I had."

"Hey, you had me," said Felicity.

"Sounds like you were all seduced by the tool of Satan," said Mike. "And *you* didn't even need a profile to be seduced, Tayler."

"And as much as I love you, Shaun, you and Tayler shouldn't be here in Astra City," Felicity cautioned. She took a sip.

"Between your couch, Mike's bed, and Shaun's spare room, I think I'm pretty safe," I replied.

The others shook their heads. That's when a blinding flash lit the room.

"What was that?" Felicity asked. "You all saw it, didn't you?"

I was already heading upstairs. Mike and Shaun followed close behind. Outside the bookstore, a few people stumbled onto the street. Some rubbed their eyes while one woman crouched next to her muscular dog, stroking its head to stop it from trembling. Through the windows of the buildings, onlookers peered like dazed hostages.

I stepped outside. A middle-aged man was near the store, clasping his eyes with his hands.

"What did you see?"

Slowly, his palms slid down his cheeks. "An orange sky."

I looked up. He was right. People took out their devices and searched for information.

"We saw a flash of light from the basement," said Shaun.

I didn't realize he was standing behind me. Felicity and Mike looked on from the doorway.

"Goth Industries," the man muttered. "First that rumble, now the devil himself painting the heavens."

"You're not serious?"

"Of course I am. Our city is going to die because of that damn uranium mine. Our city's on fire!"

"Where did you get the idea our city was on fire?"

He reached to the inside pocket of his fawn jacket and pulled out his screen, showing me an announcement the Government had made only five minutes prior.

"You've got it wrong, sir. It says the mine is on fire."

"Look at the sky, lad. Look at the sky. We'll all be dead in no time."

"None of this makes sense. It can't be real."

But my words hung like a forgotten coat in a secondhand store. The night sky was tainted orange, as if the stars were out of kilter and the sun was on its way to swallow the moon. I shielded my eyes, still seeing ginger hues through the shade.

# Twenty-Three

"WHAT'S GOING ON, Tayler?" Mike asked, as if I had all the answers.

I darted my attention between him and the strangely colored sky. The hue had faded, even though the moon still had an orange glow.

"Don't ask me how, Mike, but I'm sure the Government has something to do with this."

He stretched his arm out to the sky. "With this, Tayler? With this?"

"Stuart said he had something else in mind because our band of naughty Social Media Socialites got out of hand."

"But this?" He pulled out his screen and entered the chatrooms of the Alta Net. There were questions back and forth from mining-leak believers and nonbelievers. Mike read intently.

Shaun was comforting Felicity at the doorway of her bookstore, although she didn't seem worried.

"We have to rescue Madeline and Connor," said Shaun.

"Oh yeah?" Felicity's voice was condescending. "You and whose army?"

"They're in the hands of a madman. Tayler, don't give me that look. Whatever relationship Madi had with the Government, it may not be the same now. Remember, she helped you escape by riding—"

"Okay, Shaun," I said. "I get the picture."

More bewildered folk littered the streets. Their eyes were mostly transfixed on the red layer over their world, while some also scrolled for news. But across the road, a girl about my age in a fleecy jacket was observing me. I knew that look. She marched right up with the confidence of a scout leader.

"What do you make of this, Tayler?" she asked.

"I doubt it's Goth Industries's doing."

"Hmm." She too was dividing her time between the burning patterns on the moon and her device. I discreetly looked to see if she was logged onto the Alta Net. She was. "You're right, Tayler. You're so right. It would be a bloody big fire for us to see its effects from here."

"There's something else that doesn't add up," Felicity said. "If this fire is so intense that we're seeing it change the color of our city, why can't we feel its heat?"

"And where's the smoke?" I said. "I can't smell a thing."

The stranger nodded. "Come with me. All of you, come with me. I want to show you something."

"We don't know you," Felicity said, unusually suspicious.

Somehow I trusted her. "I'll go with you."

"I'm coming too," said Mike.

Shaun and Felicity shared a vacant glance. "We'll stay here," he said. "Contact us if you need us."

Soon we were following our unknown host through speechless individuals, either typing or staring at the heavens. I'd never known Astra City to be so eerie. Eventually, I had to turn away from the reddish sky and focus on where we were being led. In front of us, our shadows extended like anorexic giants, gazing ahead and keeping us safe.

"Why don't they leave the city if they're scared?"

"With what?" Mike replied. "No one in our neighborhood has a car."

"But if they're scared, why not walk?"

"How many people do you know who have left the city? People live their whole lives here only seeing the world through a screen in their living room, or in their hand." He looked back to his device.

"Look around you," our mysterious guide said. "Even with a spectacle like this, people still aren't talking to each other."

"Surely this is a time when you'd want to talk to the person next to you," I said. "Just to make sense of what's going on." I laughed. "Who am I to talk? I haven't even asked your name."

She walked up the stairs of a brick building. "I'm Jamie."

"I'm Mike."

She stopped, turned, and grinned. At the top of the stairs stood a man with crooked teeth. She gently slapped his palm before he opened the door for us. He watched me when I passed as if to gain a second look.

We climbed a spiral staircase to the top where a deep bass beat shook the floor. An open apartment door beckoned us to indulge in sensual delights. We stepped into a world where folk of all colors and shapes danced suggestively. Some even preferred to party topless. Several gifted women allowed guests to fondle their breasts. One nervous guy was encouraged to lick a nipple. Slight applause followed as he shared a goofy grin the moment his dare was completed.

Jamie ushered us through this mismatched cast. I caught a glimpse of several rooms on our way to the kitchen. One was full of naked men enjoying each other's delights. The next was the women-only room, followed by mixed sexes.

"What are we doing here?" Mike asked.

She went to the sink and poured a glass of tap water for each of us. "You have no idea what's happening, do you?"

"It's obviously an orgy," I replied. "Has Movie Night morphed into the ultimate human experience? I wish Shaun had come. He would be pleased."

"It's an *End of the World* party, Tayler. They're springing up all over the city. Everyone's having their last hurrah."

"This party's creeping me out."

"I thought it might, but it was something you had to see."

"Thanks, I guess." Mike stuttered a little on these words.

"I have a confession," I said. "I noticed you're on the Alta Net, Jamie."

They both shushed me in unison.

"Sorry," whispered Mike. "Tayler's new to the site."

"Why are we being quiet? We're the only ones in the kitchen."

"You don't want to be overheard when you talk about that site," she said.

"Well, where can we talk? It's refreshing to have this discussion without having to type it."

She looked around and then steered us out of the apartment and up the fire escape. We dodged someone's laundry hanging on the roof, but I took the full force of a bra I didn't see. Soon we used our devices as torches.

Music was playing from various apartments. One had a lone guy bobbing his head to a tune I couldn't make out. Another had two people swaying. And another had two making love in the living room.

Then it struck me. The sinister orange glow had gone.

"It's discussion time," Jamie declared.

"What about?"

"I'll start." Mike spoke in a low tone. "Tayler, why do you think the Government is behind this?"

"You know my reasons. I know Stuart. I don't know how he's doing it, but he's doing it."

"That doesn't prove it's the work of the Government. This drama is bringing people together, not keeping them apart."

"But in fear. Didn't you see that article on how some leaders in the past used scare tactics to control their citizens?"

"From what you've told me about Stuart, he's not the type of person who'd change tack."

"From what I've told you, he's exactly the type of person who'd change tack if something wasn't working."

"He's in power, Tayler." Mike's voice shot up. He lowered his head and continued. "What else does he need?"

"A voice. The very reason..." I glanced at Jamie. At the same time, Mike's eyes widened.

"Go on," she said.

"Perhaps this place is too open to have this conversation."

"I've got another place we can go to, one that will blow your mind." Jamie sounded as if she was enticing a trick in an alley.

"Not with more wall-to-wall sex?" Mike asked.

As Jamie took a step, she paused and said, "I've got to gain your trust. After our next stop, I think I'll win you both over."

I lowered my device to switch off the light and then noticed a ladybug at my feet. I shuffled my shoe closer to it, but it didn't move. Then I had an odd hunch. I looked up. As I raised my torch, I saw two other bugs high above us. They also stayed still. Not a wing movement. Not a careful crawl across the brickwork. I crouched.

"When did this fascination with insects begin?" Mike asked.

"About half a minute ago."

I walked my fingers carefully to its domed face. Again, no movement. I shone my light in another direction, counted to ten, and then shone it back on the bug. It didn't move. *Is it dead?*

I handed my device to Jamie and laid my palm behind the bug, nudging it forward. All I seemed to do was drag it across the surface. I touched it, lightly. It felt weird. I tapped it. Jamie squealed. It didn't squash so I scooped it up.

Close up, it seemed manufactured. I brushed it, feeling a hard plastic shell.

"Is it a toy?" Mike asked.

"I don't know what it is, but it isn't real."

"Should we take a picture and post it on the Alta Net?" Jamie asked. "Maybe someone knows what it is?"

"I don't think so." I licked my lower lip. "Who comes up to a roof?"

"People hanging clothes."

I placed the object in the change pocket of my jeans as we made our way down the stairs and onto the street. There were fewer people now and some gazed at me the more I tried to be inconspicuous. It wasn't a trait I had mastered.

Only a couple of blocks away was our destination, another rare brick building in a city of glass and steel. Jamie wandered casually through the unlocked door.

It was a vast space, yet in one corner, fake walls had been assembled. A voice was nattering away with authority, and as we ambled to the other side of the barrier, a man in a formal white shirt and black trousers addressed an audience of about thirty people all seated on strange wooden furniture.

The objects all looked as if a bench and a toolbox had spawned a litter. They were neatly placed in several rows, with two people sitting at each of these things. The man speaking at the front of this room stopped and told us to sit. Jamie sat with me, and as I ran my finger across the flat panel in front of my seat, she showed me how it lifted like a lid. I looked inside.

I ran my finger over the top of a jar with gunky contents marked Glue. Near it, a sharp metal stick was neatly placed next to a writing pad. I'd seen these in a movie. As I picked up the rod, I noticed it could bend in the middle to make the letter V. I placed the blunt end to paper; it made a smudge. I tried to write my name, but my wrist was instantly sore.

Whoosh! I twisted swiftly toward the sound. The guy in white had somehow made the noise right next to me. In his hand was a long thin object that now pointed to the floor.

"Stop goofing off, boy," he commanded.

"Huh?"

"Put the lid down."

I did.

"Now recite your three-times table."

"Huh?"

"Come on, boy. One times three equals three. Two times three equals six. Three times three equals nine."

"Four times three equals"—I counted upward from nine—"twelve." I smirked at the others, but he smacked that stick on the back of his chair and I jumped. "Ah, um. Three times five equals, um, sixteen? Sorry, I'm not sure."

"Sorry, you're not sure, what?"

"Sorry, the real answer is fifteen, I think."

"Sorry, the real answer is fifteen, what?"

I shrugged.

His weapon lashed out again. "Sorry, the real answer is fifteen, sir." He marched forward and towered over me, tapping that thing menacingly on my desk. "Stand up, boy, and think before you answer. Five times three is what?"

"Three times five is fifteen, sir. Three times six is, fifteen, sixteen, seventeen, it's eighteen, sir."

"Good. You can stop there."

"No, this is fun."

He scowled at me.

"Three times seven is twenty-one. Three times eight is twenty-four. Three times nine is…" I quietly counted on my fingers. "Three times nine is twenty-seven. And three times ten is thirty!"

The rod whacked my desk. "I told you to stop, boy. Now sit in the corner, over there."

"Why?"

Another whack.

"Okay." I sat on a seat in the corner next to a charcoal-colored board with pastel writing.

"Face the wall!"

"Why?"

He lifted his stick of terror.

"Okay." I turned.

His antics continued for another fifteen minutes or so. Jamie attempted her four-times table and one of the others tried the six-times table. Mike had to spell words and used strange little rods to write with on that charcoal board, creating more pastel-colored letters. But he too got a sore wrist. And all of them at some stage were threatened with the baton from hell.

At times, I'd peek from my corner. The others would see me but soon learned not to react or else that man would snap at them. Yet this silent camaraderie made me feel a worth I didn't recognize. A universal empathy was present, and I knew it just by sitting there. I didn't need to confirm it through typed communication.

"Class dismissed." He instantly broke out of character as some of the others got up and joined him at the front of the room, including one who looked familiar.

Jamie and Mike joined me at my spot in the corner.

"What is this?" I asked.

"School," Jamie replied.

"No, it can't be. School was never this strict when I was young."

"It's what school was like long before any of us were born."

That familiar guy was about to walk over to us, but the role-playing teacher strolled ahead.

"Welcome to your first Life Experience Mob encounter," he said.

"I thought that's who you were."

"Did you enjoy your lesson?"

"Yeah, although I feel I shouldn't have."

"What was that rod you were threatening us with?" Mike asked.

"It's a cane," he said. "If students got out of hand, they'd have to come to the front of the class and be whipped on the ass with this thing."

"In front of their friends?" I asked.

"Yes."

"On their bare ass?"

"No. They kept their pants on."

"That's immoral. This actually happened in schools?"

"A long, long time ago."

"The stuff in that weird furniture...?"

"You mean the stuff inside your desk."

"I guess so. Where did you get it?"

"We plan carefully before we make this stuff, Tayler."

I gave a sheepish grin.

"Are you surprised I know you?"

"He's used to it," Mike said, before introducing himself.

Of course, Jamie already knew our wannabe teacher who told us his name was Carter. And next to him was Hendrix, the handsome man who I first met through my work computer screen when our automated receptionist accidentally put him through to me.

"What I liked most about what just happened is that I felt things I hadn't felt before." I said. "You made me feel alive!"

"Thanks," said Hendrix. "That's our goal. Reconnection and re-education has to happen here in Astra City. People have to discover their survival skills. They also need to feel a sense of awe."

Carter gave me the type of smile my fourth-grade teacher used to whenever I got my tiny head around a new concept.

"What else have you got planned?"

"A dinner party," Carter said. "No mirror meals, no restaurants. Just a group of friends eating a three-course meal. And we'll teach one of them to cook it beforehand."

"How do you fund yourselves?"

"We ask for donations from the people who attend our sessions. Plus we've found supporters who give us money through..." He bit his bottom lip.

"Through the Alternative Network site," Jamie continued.

"And you get enough money through supporters to fund all this?"

"Tayler, we come from old money," Hendrix explained. "So we're spending mummy and daddy's wealth."

"It must cost you a fortune to research all these scenarios."

More discreet looks.

"We studied social history at university. We don't need to research much else."

"University? What's that?"

"Um, it's where rich kids go after they finish school."

I felt like I was listening to an alien life form.

"You went to school? Where?"

"Tayler, we're not from Astra City," Carter replied.

"And where you're from, they have schools?"

"And universities for more education."

"And it's not online?"

He shook his head.

"Hmm. I have another question for you."

"Go on."

"Why did you do this tonight? I mean, there was a radiation scare. An unused uranium mine was burning. Why were you doing this?"

Carter took his time replying. "Really? There was a fire?" He looked to his companion. "I guess we were too busy to realize."

Their expressions of concern were as convincing as Madi's love for me.

"Seriously? You knew nothing about it?"

"Tayler, keep quiet and listen. Hear that silence? It's pretty soundproofed in here."

"Okay then, I have another question. Why did you guys come to Astra City?"

Carter moved next to me and sat on the lid of one of those old-fashioned desks.

"Like Hendrix said, because the people in your city need our services." He seemed preoccupied for a moment, then observed me as he continued. "Yes, the people in your city are encouraged to have the same view, unlike generations before them who talked to each other. They met people in the course of life whose views confronted them, made them reconsider, and move forward through understanding those around them. That's why social gatherings like dinner parties were important. That's how people conquered their fears.

"Now opposing views are frowned upon on Social Media Central, because opposing views can go as far as being the polar opposite, like a rubber band stretching back and forth. And once people are switched off to other views, they're scared of the people who hold them. You see, the danger social media poses is that more people are prepared to venture down paths to others who agree with them, through their own rabbit holes never to return. It is the fastest way to change and rearrange alliances."

"And that's what we're doing, with the Alta Net?"

"Don't mistake my meaning. I wasn't referencing the Alta Net just then."

"So how can they venture down other paths if opposing views are frowned upon?" I really didn't need to hear the answer. All this made sense from what I'd seen.

"If they don't live in Astra City, they can. Freely and readily." Someone in the room called Carter's name. "Come and meet some of the others in our group."

"I want to stay here and talk to Hendrix," I replied. "If that's okay with you?"

Hendrix nodded.

Mike eyed me warily, but Jamie took his arm and led him to meet the others. Carter followed.

"You want to know what that work call was about, don't you, Tayler?"

"Hell, yes. Something about something that didn't work properly?"

"I can't talk about it."

"Are you an engineer, Hendrix?"

"Tayler!"

"You were building some new toy for AV Enterprises."

He made a gesture as if zipping his lips shut.

"If you don't want to say anything, then why did you agree to stay here to talk?"

"Because I need to tell you that what I was working on, I'm no longer part of. And that in your highly regarded celebrity position, you shouldn't ask questions."

"Come on. You can't just leave me in the dark."

"Trust me. We're... I'm protecting you."

"What are you doing in Astra City?"

"We told you. To help bring real-life experiences to the people here."

"Yes, I know. But what about you in particular? What did you come here to work on?"

"Stop asking!"

I had a hunch. I fished around in my pocket for that ladybug and held it to his face. "You mentioned sound, but somehow the light projections didn't work."

"Please, it needs to be destroyed!" He reached out to take it from my hand, but I quickly popped it back in my pocket.

"I think someone else finally got the projection to work."

Mike called out, "We've got to go."

I blew him a kiss to quell his troubled expression.

"So soon?" Carter asked.

Jamie studied both Mike and me. "I think we should go."

I hadn't noticed that drinks were being poured and that some of the small group were already enjoying refreshments crowded around their antique desks.

But like a concerned older sister, Jamie marched in my direction to collect me. Hendrix kept his gaze and shook his head steadily as I walked away. We bid our new buddies farewell and promised to return for another session. We were told to check the Alta Net for dates and times. I walked out of the warehouse with two emotions competing for dominance. One was a sense of pride I couldn't comprehend. The other was clarity although there were still some unanswered motives.

The three of us wandered the night streets alone, our footsteps echoing like a single drumbeat. And for a moment, a lone dog barked in the distance as if calling to us.

"You're walking with your head in the clouds," said Jamie.

"Who, me?" I felt a goofy grin emerge. "You're right. For the first time in my life, I feel empowered. Like there's hope for humanity."

That dog howled, its frantic voice coming closer as we made our way up the block.

"Suddenly, the city feels eerie again," Mike noted.

We halted and listened for its cries.

"Hear that?" Jamie asked.

"Yes. That dog is whimpering now."

She ran ahead. We followed, picking up pace to catch her. Soon, we were at the building where the sex party was located. That man was no longer guarding the door, but at the foot of the steps, the dog was chasing its tail. Its voice had diminished, and in its panicked state, it was too preoccupied to notice us. We raced upstairs.

Blood trailed across the carpet inside the apartment. Only several half-naked individuals were left, cowering at the dining table.

"They killed themselves," said one before we had time to query.

"Who?" Jamie said.

"An older couple. They didn't want to be killed by radiation. So they ended it. They ended it in front of everyone."

Then I noticed a gun on the table.

Mike grabbed my hand. "We have to get out of here. We can't be here when the police arrive."

He pulled me backward. All color drained from Jamie's face.

"Come with us," I called.

"I can't," she replied. "This is my apartment."

# Twenty-Four

I WOKE AT Mike's. He wasn't in bed with me, so I called his name. No reply. I jumped out of bed, naked, and ran to the window. The sun shone brightly. In the street below, a few folk plodded along as if they were sleep deprived. I grabbed my jeans from the floor.

As I pulled them on, a small lump rode up my leg. The ladybug! I slipped on a T-shirt before I fished the object from my change pocket.

In the daylight, it was redder than I remembered. I laid it on the edge of Mike's writing desk and crouched so I could view it from eye level. I tapped it, confirming it was plastic. I tipped it on its back and fondled its feet. They were stiff, unable to be moved.

I scooped it into my palm before pinching it between two fingers and bringing it to Mike's computer screen. I pushed gently on its back, making it grip the monitor.

"Wow," I whispered to myself.

I grabbed my device, turned on its camera, and zoomed in on the insect as closely as I could. I noted the perfect line on its back. And that's when it happened. I moved in too close and bumped it, losing sight of it.

*Why is a writer's desk such an obstacle course?*

I was focused between the loose sheets of paper and the edge of the tray they were sitting in. I reached in, carefully feeling between the gap.

"Ouch."

Paper cut. I sucked my fingertip, taking in the metallic taste of my own blood. The pain was equal parts agony and annoyance, so I hurried to the tap and let water soothe my wound. It was then I saw it.

On the hardwood floor were two small specks, both red and black. I rushed back with my finger still wet. The ladybug had split in two. I scooped up the parts and placed them side by side on the desk. I went back to turn the tap off and find a Band-Aid.

When I hovered over the pieces in zoom mode once again, I noted a V-shape protruding from one, and an inverted V inside the other. These shapes were two parts of a microchip inside whatever this ladybug was supposed to be. I clicked the pieces together. The insect replica was intact again. I snapped the pieces apart. No damage. I clicked them together. It lay on my palm as I brought it closer to my eyes.

*Fascinating.*

I pulled the pieces apart again and studied the protruding side of the chip. Tiny lettering marked its underside. I held that thing close to my device as I was determined to bring those letters into focus.

"Av ent," I read out loud. "What the frig is avent?" I turned off my zoom. "You fool, Tayler. AV Enterprises." I shut my eyes. "First, I'm told to work from home, next toy insects. How did an open-minded guy like Hendrix get caught up in my company?"

I heard someone coming up the stairs followed by the jingle of keys in the lock. Mike walked in.

"You're up. Why are you standing at my desk? Were you looking at home movies on Lover Net?"

"Very funny."

"Then why are you standing doing nothing?"

"Come over here."

I held one half of the ladybug to his face as he approached, and pointed to the other half on his desk.

"You split the ladybug in two?"

"It broke."

He tilted his head as he looked inside.

"What the—"

"Guess what else."

"What?"

"It was made for the company I worked at."

"So why didn't you recognize it last night?"

"I've never seen it before."

"Then how do you know—"

"Read the letters inside."

"Av Ent?"

"AV Enterprises."

"Oh. What does it do?"

"I have a hunch, but I'm sure that Hendrix guy from the Life Experience Mob knows for sure."

"Huh?"

"It's a long story, but I met him before through work."

"We could go to the next session and ask him."

"I tried to bring it up last night, but he was secretive about what he was doing for AV Enterprises."

I took the other half and snapped the two pieces together.

"Bring it," Mike said.

"Where?"

"To the library."

"The what?"

"We're going to the library."

"What on earth is a library?"

SHE STOOD AT a desk in a small room and was as curious about me as I was with her.

"Come. Sit. I've been waiting for you."

"You've been waiting for me?"

"No, Tayler," said Mike. "I made this appointment."

She ushered us in, then gestured to two tan lounge chairs with stitching similar to a continental quilt. Each wall of this room had shelves, and up until this point, the most shelves I'd ever seen in one room was in Felicity's bookstore. But there were no books here. Just countless larger devices hiding the walls.

"Are they for sale?"

"Excuse him, Christine. This is a new experience for him."

"At least he's here experiencing it. Most people wouldn't know this place exists."

"If they're not for sale, what are they for?" I was feeling like an outsider for the first time in ages.

"Pick one up and turn it on," the woman said. Her angular haircut bobbed as she talked.

I reached over and chose one randomly. I opened the flap that hid its screen, then switched it on. No SMC logo appeared. No Alta Net symbol, either. A numbering system materialized instead, and as the numbers kept darting in from the left of the screen, words slipped in to join them from the right. It was crude animation.

"What have we logged onto?"

"Nothing," she replied. "What you're seeing is stored inside the device itself. Go on, tap one of the numbers."

I did. An article popped up on the screen in lifeless monochrome. I read the first three paragraphs.

"What's the matter?" Mike asked.

"What's a journalist?"

"I don't know. Christine, what's a journalist?"

"A reporter. Oh, for heaven's sake, someone who goes out and finds news."

"So at any time, anyone of us is a journalist?" I was seeking clarification.

She pressed her wrinkled finger on the screen. "This story is about a famous journalist. Well, he was famous at one time, when journalists practiced the art of journalism."

"Did he write blogs?" Mike asked.

She looked weary, although her eyes weren't red.

"My dear baby-minded chums, once upon a time, people were paid to sit at typewriters, I mean laptops, no, something that they could write with, after going out and interviewing other people about the day's events. They'd have secret discussions, then come back and let all of us know what was going on, fairly or unfairly, in the town or the city or even the world."

"Wow," I said. "And they were paid to do this? Oh."

"What's that look for?"

"Did they write for *Gazettes* and *Chronicles*?"

"Yes, they did. And for *Heralds* and *Times*."

"So people were paid to write for these things. They didn't do it for free. Oh wow." I faced Mike. "Are we here to read these things?"

"No. We're here to talk to Christine."

We both swiveled our chairs to face her.

"I'm glad you rang me, Mike, but I didn't feel comfortable answering your questions through my device. And quite frankly, you're not the only one who's come here to see me about this."

"About what?" I asked.

"Goth Industries never existed," he replied.

"How can you be sure?"

Christine ran her finger across one row of devices. "In these electronic journals are the history of Astra City, Beta City, and Cradle Edge. A team of us have flipped through every article to do with mining and industry. We worked around the clock for days, and nowhere did we find any mention of a uranium mine."

"But does that really prove Goth didn't exist?"

"I'm old enough to have seen all this information, which was once at everybody's fingertips through the click of a mouse, be transferred from its public site to the all-knowing Social Media Central. It became law. No other internet site was allowed to exist."

"And people were okay with that?"

"Back then, SMC wasn't only a site for people to put up futile thoughts and pointless photos. We were glad it helped centralize so much information in a way that bled into forums and discussions more easily. Someone just had to write a word, and the side of their screen would be filled with related articles. But bit by bit this information, like much of the world's knowledge, simply disappeared. It wasn't sudden. It was a gradual thing."

"But that doesn't mean Goth didn't exist."

"I don't remember Goth Industries or a uranium mine, and I've been around for quite a few years. And trust me, my mind is as sharp as a tack."

"Are you sure? Maybe the mine was kept secret."

"Maybe it was. That's why the others in my team have gone searching for it. They set out on foot yesterday."

"Is that safe?"

"We believe so, because we're ninety-nine percent sure it's fiction."

I swiveled to face Mike. "She's right. I know she's right. This has Stuart's fingerprints, and some of Hendrix's, all over it."

"That's why I brought you here, Tayler."

I gazed at the wealth of information on the walls. "Whose devices are these?"

"They are what's left of Astra City's library. People used to visit and read at their leisure."

"What people?"

"Lots of people. When I was going to school—"

"Don't mention school to Tayler," Mike said. "He's envious of your generation."

My lips clenched.

"Anyway, when I was at school, I'd visit the library to do my homework, but the library was much bigger then. And people were paid to work there. Now a handful of us have the key to what's left in this room and let people visit when they want."

"But if this information used to be available through Social Media Central, then erased through some illogical whim of the Government of the day, it means that these journals are probably illegal."

She gently took the device from my fingers and clutched it to her chest.

"That's why, my dear boys, Stuart has no idea this library exists."

# Twenty-Five

I STEPPED OUTSIDE of Shaun's block and shut my eyes. The afternoon sun reached out to me and spread its warmth across my face. I had to feel this. It was a suggestion from the Alta Net on a page where my connections were posting their simple pleasures.

Its rays shot through my body as I took off my shirt. This fiery sphere offered this service nearly every day, and here I was, taking advantage of its glow for the first time in my life. I swear, I felt vitamin D penetrate every organ inside me.

And then I stopped analyzing. I was bathed in nature's blanket. Serene with each thought. Revitalized through meditation.

Time marched on, but I wasn't moving. Shaun joined me.

"Where are you?"

"I don't know, but I'm not coming back. Shit! What's that?"

Sirens sounded through Astra City, and while neither of us knew where they were coming from, I could tell one was very near. I felt the vibration through my legs. And it all made sense to me.

Some people were running to shelter, while others pointed and laughed at the scared. As could be expected, everyone was checking their device.

A small girl covered her ears, pushing tightly so not even a whisper could enter. Her mother picked her up and shielded her face. Then she trembled. No frame of reference prepared her for this.

Then abruptly, the sirens ceased.

We went inside. Mike was seated while Felicity hunched over the lounge, watching his screen over his shoulder.

As we huddled over, I saw the strangest font behind the glass. An authoritarian font, if one could exist, spelled out:

STANDBY FOR A MESSAGE FROM THE GOVERNMENT

Next to it, a series of numbers counted backward. It took me a moment to realize that in ninety seconds we would hear from my nemesis.

"Connor and Madeline are being entertained by a madman," said Shaun.

I pulled out my device and went to Social Media Central. All eyes turned to me as I realized that none of this site was accessible except for the page we were already looking at on Mike's screen.

I brought up the Alta Net, but as I was about to log in as John24, Stuart Manning appeared on Mike's screen. That burgundy jacket I once admired draped his frame with conviction. The coat of arms behind him added to the image of someone playing dictator, a word I had only just discovered through the alternative net.

He began to speak. "Citizens of Astra City, I need to tell you something. I need to tell you to stop killing yourselves. The tragic suicide of Edgar and Mavis Stephenson was without cause, and we don't need anyone else taking their own lives. Trust me, I know what I'm saying. And who am I? Some of you won't have a clue. I am the Government."

He looked down, as if he was reading from something off-screen. He shook his head and faced us again.

"Let me say this in my own words. First off, I am in power, although many of you don't understand what power I have. I am your leader. I *have* been for a while.

"And for those concerned about radiation, don't worry, we have things under control. This old uranium mine is not going to kill us. I've been speaking to other leaders and experts from many cities and they are offering help."

"How?" I mumbled.

"I thought you didn't believe any of this was real," said Felicity.

"So don't kill yourselves, citizens," the madman continued. "The mess left by Goth Industries will no longer be our burden."

A different image appeared on this live stream. We were faced with film of tired faces confined to metal-framed beds. Their skin hung off their cheekbones like bedsheets blown backward on the clothesline. Their eyes bulged, and while we watched, Stuart's commanding voice continued.

"We are tending the sick with the help of our neighboring cities. But please read our precautions through the link I'll give you after this message. And stay glued to Social Media Central for all the latest news on this crisis."

"Oh my..." I said.

"It's, it's..." Shaun added, just as lost for words as I was.

Both Connor and Madi were on the screen, as pale as white ash. Her once-confident eyes looked away from the camera, like a child avoiding eye contact not sure if she was in trouble. And Connor kept his eyelids closed as if this was an intrusion.

"She's still doing Stuart's bidding," I said.

"Not by choice. Madeline never looks that bad for anyone. She's being forced into it."

Half of me knew this was true, but the other half didn't want to be taken for a fool again.

"What great publicity," said Felicity. "Using the fallen to spike interest in yourself."

"But Stuart hijacked SMC," Mike noted. "It wouldn't matter who or what he showed us, he had everyone's full attention."

A link appeared at the bottom of the screen. Mike tapped it. The social media profile for the Government came up. All the standard Like, Share, and Follow buttons were present, and as we watched, the small counters next to them raced up into their thousands.

I continued logging onto the Alta Net. About a hundred or so connections had asked me what I made of this chaos. Others were curious what I thought of Connor and Madeline Q being among the sick. I still maintained it was a sham.

I turned to Shaun. "We have to get Madi and Connor out of there."

"But you can't just barge in," Mike cautioned.

The sound of heavenly harps shot up my body.

"What's in your pants?" Felicity asked.

I squeezed out the plastic ladybug. It echoed the music around Shaun's living room. It was so loud, I tossed the thing onto the kitchen counter. It bounced into the sink, causing the steel to vibrate.

"What is that?" Shaun asked.

He took a step toward it, then stopped and listened. We all kept quiet, realizing that the classical tune was not just inside the apartment. Then his kitchen was bathed in mauve light.

"Exactly as I suspected," I declared. "Projection. Sound. Hendrix. Everyone, outside!"

People studied the skies as if all answers appeared from the blue. But this time, some of the sky was purple, as if someone had painted the heavens.

This entertaining oddity was bringing more folk out on the streets than I realized lived within the city's steel structures. My device buzzed. It was Jamie. She was streaming live on her Alta Net profile, Carter standing in front of her camera. As he began to speak, the music of the harps around me faded, and his voice echoed around the city.

"Hi. I represent a group who call ourselves the Life Experience Mob. I beg you, please don't fret. You've seen this technology before."

Although some people shrieked, curiosity soon became the mass emotion of the moment.

"On behalf of my crew, I have a confession. We created the myth of Goth Industries. Those rumbles you've heard. The orange skies. It was us. We were commissioned to do it."

He looked upward, pausing and frowning a little.

"Watch this."

The strange color disappeared. Then green took over, spilling some of its hue onto the streets. And just as quickly, it vanished.

"Now listen," Carter said, his voice still echoing around the buildings.

And there was that rumble that first scared everyone when I went through my madness wearing underwear in the park.

No one flinched. The chime of harps returned under his voice.

"On behalf of myself and my team, I'm begging your forgiveness. This was all meant to be a game, at least that's what we were told. We wanted it to be the mystery in your lives that would bring you together, not separate you back to your world of screens.

"We didn't want to be another event on your social media platform. We wanted to be the thing that made you feel something. We wanted to spark your imaginations. We wanted you to talk and connect.

"But two people took our message to heart, and for that, we are truly sorry. You see, it was the Government's idea to promote ourselves this way. We wanted to bring an event into your lives, then we were going to introduce ourselves through the technology I'm using to talk to you now. The next step was to encourage you to try one of our live experiences. But I fear now we would have been silenced before our introduction."

Even more people came out of their cocoons, forcing everyone to make room on the streets. I was about to follow when Shaun held me back.

"You're too famous," he whispered. "Let *them* watch and listen."

"This was our plan," Carter's voice continued. "The Government insisted on making the story of Goth Industries more believable with that history page on SMC. We went along with it. But as for those sad images of people lying in bed, we had nothing to do with it. We'd never take it to that extreme, especially in light of the tragic suicides. It's confirmed what we suspected for a while now. The Government was not working with us. He was using us."

Carter's eyes were teary.

"Citizens of Astra City, you need to connect in the real world, just like Tayler and the Social Media Socialites were trying to get you to do. You have to feel the rain. You have to taste a home-cooked meal prepared by a neighbor. You should challenge your friends to a game played on a board, not on a screen. But above all, don't listen to the Government. He's out to get something he hasn't got, and it's not in your best interests to let him have it."

This riddle made people's faces contort like torture victims. The harps faded, but the crowd was in no rush to go back inside.

Jamie's live stream ended. Without hesitation, I found an image of myself to upload as John24's new profile picture. I erased my description and replaced it with "By the way, I'm Tayler. Yes, that Tayler." Next, I added one of those funky GPS icons so my connections would know how to find me, face to face.

"Where are you, Tayler?" Felicity said.

"Off in my own thoughts."

"You're coming out of the closet as Tayler," said Shaun. "Is that wise?"

"For the first time in my life, I like Tayler. He's intelligent. He's brave. And he has a voice."

"Are you sure you're not just a new breed of Social Media Socialite?" Felicity asked.

"I don't know. I really don't know. But this feels right." I glanced at the sky. "Shaun, we need to rescue Madi and Connor."

He high-fived me. Felicity didn't say anything, but I was sure I noticed a tiny grin. We ventured back inside.

"What's made you change your mind about Madeline?"

"She helped me escape. Sure, she had to have sex in front of me and break my heart, but in her own way, she showed she cared for me, as twisted as that sounds."

"When did you come to that realization?" Mike asked, his voice monotone.

"It crept up on me. It's an acknowledgement, that's all." I turned to Shaun. "So what's the plan?"

"You've got a gun," he replied.

"How did you know?"

"We all know," Felicity said.

"Do you really think I never clean my apartment?" said Shaun.

"No one cleans the top of a wardrobe. Maybe once a year, but not often."

"It was me," Felicity said. "I changed the sheets in the spare bedroom, then decided to keep cleaning. I asked Shaun about the gun, but he didn't know it was there. So we thought it might be yours."

"Why didn't you leave it at my place?" Mike asked.

"You're more likely to clean." I laughed. "If you all thought I planted a gun in the spare bedroom, why didn't you ask me about it?"

"You were unstable at the time," Felicity replied. "So we thought it best not to ask. By the way, I moved it so you wouldn't do anything rash."

She went to the laundry and fished around the cleaning products. Soon she returned with the weapon.

"Why didn't you just tell us you had it?"

"Like you said, I *was* unstable. I didn't want you to think I'd do something stupid with it."

"It's impressive." Mike studied it.

"Boys and their toys," Felicity moaned.

"You know what we're like."

"So what's the plan?" I asked.

"Let's head down to Stuart's compound and work it out from there," Shaun said. "You still remember the way, don't you, Tayler?"

"Clearly."

"Boys, their toys, and their stupid bravado," Felicity moaned.

"We can't do nothing."

"Tayler's right, we can't," said Shaun.

"Well, if that's the case, I'm coming with you," said Felicity.

"No, you're not. I don't want anything happening to you."

"Likewise. But if I'm with you, there's less chance of you trying to be brave."

"Aren't you scared?" I asked.

She peered down her nose. "After seeing that spectacle outside and that Stuart guy on the screen, of course not. The Government is merely a little man looking for a platform."

"He has guards."

She clasped her hands against her chin. "Hmm."

"I'm coming with you," Mike declared. "I agree with Felicity. Stuart Manning is a charlatan. And the Life Experience Mob have humiliated him. They've got him by the balls. Now's our chance to strike."

An ear-splitting zap rendered us speechless. We stood huddled together, trying to work out the source of an electro buzzing sound. I rushed to the window and saw crimson sparks shooting from the front door of the apartment building. Soon, Shaun's front doorknob began to melt as trickles of hot metal scorched the door on their way down.

"It's going to burn," said Felicity.

That's when I noticed a black limousine waiting outside.

"He's here," I gasped.

The smoke started to build, but as the flames began, a white gas poured through the smoldering cracks in the door, killing the fire stone dead.

One kick and the doorway was free of obstruction. The Government and his driver stood like villains from a comic strip, their odd tools chucked to one side.

"Don't fret, children," said the loathsome man. "It's Tayler we want."

"You have an unhealthy obsession with me."

"With you and John24. Oh, don't give me that look, boy. I have my fingers in many pies."

"Stuart, he's no harm to you." It would have made sense if Shaun said this, but he didn't. Even Felicity would have been a better choice for the voice of reason. Of all people in the room, Mike spoke up.

"Mike, your father, Bernard, says hello."

Mike stood wavering, as if deciding whether or not to jump off a cliff. I must have looked the same. And while each jigsaw piece fell into place, I still was grappling with the facts.

Bernard, the fake social-media friend I had stumbled into at the compound. Mary, whose heart he played with on Lover Net. And now I made my identity known on the alternative site introduced to me by Mike. *I remember Bernard saying he had a son but did he mention his name?* But here was Stuart Manning at my side like a leech impossible to get rid of.

"And you doubted me when I told you about the secret compound, Mike," I said. "Yet you must have known about it all along."

"Tayler, you threw me off guard. Shit, I have feelings for you. How could I tell you that I knew all along?"

Note to self. Never fall in love, lust or anything in between.

I cleared my throat. "Government, I'm all yours."

# Twenty-Six

ALL THE WAY back to the compound, he made me watch a site called "Tayler on Trial" on my device.

"Really? What am I on trial for?"

"Treason."

"Seriously? No one on Social Media Central has ever heard of that crime."

"Well, the guilty verdict is rising."

"With complete accuracy, I'm sure." I leaned forward to see his smug face, but he never looked my way. "Why did you come for me? I mean, the Life Experience Mob is who you should be after."

"We are." Finally he took off his seat belt and peered at me from the passenger seat. "But they've gone into hiding. Who knows if they're even in Astra City anymore? Their warehouse is vacated."

"So you decided to come for me instead."

"Tut-tut, child. I'm not the only one interested in you. It seems Madeline also has some unfinished business."

"How is she? How is Connor?"

"You'll see for yourself soon enough."

I leaned back into my seat. The city was vacant again. With all the confessions, lies, and spectacle of the day, it was as if no one cared. It was evening, the perfect time for flirting and a mirror meal. Or maybe someone was in a restaurant. Maybe someone was making love in person and not through a camera. Maybe it was just me who felt alone.

I checked my device for what I felt would give me comfort. An image that would give me strength for whatever Stuart was about to make me face. I flicked a few photos and found it. That selfie with me, Madi, Connor and Candy. We all looked happy, or more to the point, Candy looked happy. The rest of us looked relieved.

*Why that bikie thinks Madi looks jealous of Candy is beyond me.*

I shut my eyes and pressed the picture against my chest. Someone's death had to be avenged. Yes, that sounded like a reason as to why I gave myself up to re-enter Stuart's lair, even if I had trouble believing it.

I glanced at the selfie again. I had no idea if I would see tomorrow.

*Whatever I'm about to face, Candy, please help me through this.*

We eventually made it to the compound. Businesslike guards. Soulless metal construction. Echoes bounced back at headache-inducing levels. And as Stuart walked by my side, my stomach quivered.

"My chance to be Astra City's hero has now gone down the gurgler. You and people like you, want to enlighten people. They're only sheep, boy. They're the great unwashed. You saw that for yourself when you brushed with fame."

Another metal door slid open. At the end of the corridor lay Madi and Connor in their beds. She looked up and grinned momentarily, while Connor's tired eyes widened.

"Here are your colleagues," Stuart said snidely. "Why don't you play for a while?"

Connor growled back, but Stuart had already turned away, his burgundy jacket adding the pizzazz he lacked.

"Hug me, Tayler," Connor requested. "I'm not getting up. I'm conserving my energy."

"Haven't they been feeding you?"

"He refuses to eat," Madi replied.

I passed two video cameras mounted to the wall, then crouched and held my friend. I loosened my grip when I heard him gasp. He cupped the back of my head with his hand and drew me affectionately into his chest.

"What's going on, Connor? Why is Stuart doing this?"

"To give the appearance of power." His voice became raspy.

"But he's the Government. He has power. None of his actions make sense."

"We know," said Madeline.

"Thank you for helping me escape," I said to my ex.

"It's the least I could do after what I put you through."

"You can say that again."

"Be kind to her, Tayler," Connor gasped. "Notice how she's in here with me and not with that self-deluded idiot out there."

I drifted to her.

"I could say a thousand things, but I'd never regain your trust." Solemn was not a look she wore well.

"Try me."

Connor gave her a wink. A little glamour shone through her fatigue.

She lowered her voice. "I was never supposed to sleep with you."

"Great way to start an apology, Madeline Q."

"Please hear me out. Yes, I was supposed to recruit you into our team—"

"Why me?"

"As Stuart told you over that banquet, you were his model geek. A demographic of Astra City he wasn't getting his message through to, although apparently it wasn't his idea."

"Whose was it?"

She shrugged. "As I was saying, I never was supposed to sleep with you, but you touched something inside."

"Warning, cliché coming on," said Connor.

"Shut up," she sniped. "You're sick."

"Trust me, this is lifting my spirits."

"Tayler, ignore him. I need to say this. And he's right, it is a cliché but you did touch something inside me. You must have known it yourself. You knew the point when my flirting became attraction."

"Yes, I did. The moment you saw me as a person rather than a nerd."

"You were never a nerd, my love. It just took me time to see it. Once I did, I discovered the world inside Tayler. And I discovered the world inside Madi, not Madeline Q."

"Oh brother." Connor rolled his eyes.

"Shh," I said. "Let the girl speak."

She sniffled. "I'm trying not to cry." It didn't work. A few tears found their way down her cheeks. "I'm a silly girl." She wiped away the moisture with the back of her hand. "I never meant to hurt you. Hell, I never meant to fall in love with you. But I did. I took a step too far. And now we're here. Three peas in a pod in a lunatic's lair."

"That's poetic, Madi. I've never known you to talk like that."

"Try sharing a cell with Connor for as long as I have. It rubs off on you, lover."

"And here we are, alive," he said. "Candy's not, but for some reason, we're alive."

"As heartless as this sounds, we're just too valuable. If he wants to kill us, it has to be an event on Social Media Central. We won't perish quietly in this compound."

"No, you won't perish quietly in this compound," Stuart announced from the door, flanked by two guards. "Come, come. It's primetime for the city folk on SMC."

"We never got to talk about Shaun and Felicity," Connor murmured. I helped him to his feet.

"There's so much more I need to tell you. Stuart has been publicly shamed."

"What?"

"Shh. Let's see what this madman wants."

To my astonishment, the two guards came forward to help Connor. I helped Madi from her bed, but as she took her first few steps, I realized her health was okay. Two extra guards instantly appeared to march us through the compound. We were heading for the exit I had escaped from, but before we came to that door, we stood outside the room that streamed fake friendships to the citizens of Astra City.

"This is it, isn't it, Madeline?" Connor asked.

"Yep, here it is."

That clueless girl was supervising again and looked up briefly from her device to frown at me. All sorts of voices trickled out, all pretending to be mysterious strangers, potential lovers, or confiding friends.

"The electronic age is a wonderful thing, my pupils," Stuart announced. "Here are our multiple living rooms, bedrooms, and studies. Once we knew we weren't being heard through your band of Social Media Socialites, we siphoned the public into smaller groups so we could reach them with more precision."

"How far back did you plan this?"

Madi and Connor frowned at me.

"Hey, I'm curious."

"Back in the days when I was the CEO of Social Media Central. I saw its potential to fool people. So once I slid into politics, I built this place with my own money."

"Hey, hold on," said Madi. "You told us you hired us first, then went to this as Plan B."

"This was Plan A until a few colleagues noticed you, Connor, and Shaun making a name for yourselves. We thought you'd be cheaper. But mass communication doesn't always work."

"You never told me any of this," Madi shrieked. "You seduced me as a Plan B!" She looked to me. "Sorry, Tayler."

"It's okay. I get it. You screwed him, but you loved me. I'm okay with that."

Stuart grinned.

I stepped forward, examining his face closely. "There's something else I'm curious about."

"How we hooked up?"

I rolled my eyes. "How do you match your employees with the fools of the outside world?"

"It's about the tone of someone's voice. We know what emotions they have by analyzing their voice patterns. We have the software to give us a personal blueprint of an individual. We know who's confident, who gets depressed, who falls for sad stories, or who feels very little. We also know who questions and who believes, so we know who to discredit. We know what they need for validation, so we know who they need from our list of employees. The employees who are also analyzed without consent. For example, displaced arty types were your Social Media Socialites audience, but you were all just part of a much larger game."

"But why go to that much trouble?" Connor asked.

"Because I'm trying to make it onto the board of the World Bank. You see, I had to control the conversations Astra City was having, and to do that, I had to control information."

"Incredible," I muttered, trailing off on the last syllable.

"Who do you think finances Astra City's services? Who do you think looks after water, electricity, manufacturing, the food laboratories, all business? It is the bank, those faceless men I'm trying to be part of."

"It's what I suspected," said Connor. "The Government has no control. The bank leads. He follows."

"Tayler, you look perplexed. Little man, all governments change their citizens' reality, whether it's to create heroes, to tell them they have an enemy, or convince them theirs is a peace-loving district. It's up to us to create that illusion, and SMC was the tool we were given."

"By who?"

"The World Bank. I have a ladder to climb, which started when I was CEO of Social Media Central."

I couldn't say anything. My forehead felt cold, then my hands. Madi sidled up and held me.

"And people dare not question your view or hear an opposing point of view," Connor said. "It's the total opposite of what the internet was all about—a worldwide conversation."

"Tsk-tsk, Camera Man, you know we can't have that. Too many people forming opinions. Hordes of individuals with different ideologies not listening to each other, not meeting on middle ground. And that middle ground has to be mine."

"So when we went way off message—"

"You were punished."

"Then you took the life of an innocent girl."

"And eventually, I will take *your* lives, but I need to make your court cases seem real. Otherwise, I'll never be on that board." He stared at me as if he was shooting a death ray from his pupils. "Oh, Tayler, you still look lost. For my plan to work, I have to stay in the background and make it look like justice is prevailing of its own accord. You're my puppets, but I can't be seen to be pulling the strings. I have to prove to the bank that I have control over my citizens and they won't wake up from their slumber anytime soon."

"We can say anything you want," Madi shrieked. "We don't have to die."

"Of course you have to die. You all know too much. And Tayler's tried to get the truth out there. Once I took poverty away from all of you, you had time to think, and now you're dangerous to me. But I have to discredit you in the public eye, or I can kiss that seat on the board goodbye. And I want that power. Money's the only real power left in the world."

Stuart gestured to a smaller room opposite. We all stepped through the steel door when it opened, and as I watched it slide shut behind us, I was being overpowered by too many emotions.

He offered us seats as the guards helped Connor to sit. We looked into the open doorways of three tinier compartments. Each gave the appearance they had been furnished from discarded items left on the street, yet the sleekest computers sat facing the distasteful fixtures.

And for some reason, I was trying to factor the Inner Knowledge Net, the idiocy of Goth Industries and our rebellious streaming telecast. All of these chaotic plans were providing clarity. Clarity about Stuart. And all confirmed what he did next.

Stuart took a few sheets of paper from the nearest table and handed one to each to us. All four guards stayed in the room as we scanned our scripts.

"You want us to read this?" I smirked. "You really are clutching at straws."

"No, don't read it. Just live it."

"They're not going to believe we're all in hiding because we spoke our minds."

"That's not what it says, Tayler."

"But it's what it implies, Stuart. The public already know the radiation sickness was a sham."

"They do?" Madi asked.

"That's why you're going to talk about the murder," said Stuart.

"The public won't believe we're all in hiding because we had something to do with it," I argued.

"The evidence, the confessions, and the trial have already happened."

"Stuart, you're so busy orchestrating a *fake* world, you've lost touch with the real one. The public already see through this continually changing narrative."

"The public have short attention spans, and they're forgetting more with each generation." He gestured to the hideous *fake* rooms. "The public believe what is streamed."

"Or ignore it totally," said Connor. "Like they did with your messages."

"And you've lost all power now, thanks to the Life Experience Mob," I added.

"The what?"

"I'll explain later."

"Tayler, real leadership ended as mass social media took off," said Stuart. "You would have read that for sure. People began posting and responding to each other directly, ignoring what was important—Government. Half a century ago, the mundane became the celebrated. Anyone and everyone had a voice, and they used it to talk about their favorite subject—themselves. Then we had to scramble to stay in power and keep you all under control. We sold ourselves like the brand of alcohol you most desire. The more you ignored democracy, the more we realized we could simply stay in power by rigging elections."

"And rigging trials," Connor added.

"Regardless, over the next month, you will use one room each as if you're in hiding. You'll find your old followers on SMC, or the Alta Net in Tayler's case, and tell them how you lost your way and how you're now scared for your life."

"So you're using our fear to control the people," said Madi. "Why would you do that?"

"Because *fear* almost worked for him," I said. "The huge hoax about radiation sickness had the public scared and ready to listen, but the people responsible for the smoke and mirrors came clean. They had to. A married couple committed suicide."

Stuart cleared his throat. "Seriously, those suicides were no reason for those jerks to admit they created the smoke and mirrors!" He spat out each syllable.

"Seriously, think this through. Why would you trust us to say what you want us to say? It didn't work before."

"Because your every word will be monitored, and if you don't stick to the plan, you'll meet the same fate as Candy. So make this charade all the more real."

"And when the public doesn't buy our idiotic confessions, what on earth could you try next? I mean, for goodness sake, man, I can smell your desperation."

He raised the back of his hand and stepped toward me but was interrupted as the door shot open. Another guard stormed into the room, so he beat him instead. Under the sickening smack, I could hear my name being chanted. Both Madi and Connor smirked, gazing at me as if I was a deity worthy of worship. As the chorus of "Tayler" seeped into our realm, the Government clutched his chest as if he was about to throw up.

"What is going on?" he asked, as the guard struck the floor. "Answer me, you lowly creature!"

The other guards swallowed as if they were stopping words from escaping their throats. He sneered at them, then kicked their wounded comrade in the stomach. One pointed his gun at Stuart, but the others quickly shot the rebel. His disloyal body shook on the floor.

"We have no time for this," said Stuart. "What's going on?"

The bruised guard spat his answer through blood.

"What did you say? I don't understand you?"

He lurched forward, speaking louder. "Sir, we have a problem."

# Twenty-Seven

"COME WITH ME!" Stuart commanded.

But we were already heading outside, minus the injured. The remaining guards once again helped Connor stumble out the exit.

Mike was at the front of the pack of about a hundred individuals. Shaun held the gun I stole while Felicity stood proudly by his side. The guy who asked John24 for advice on romance held his hand over his heart. The girl my avatar debated with constantly, about the ways civilization had declined during the generation before us, blew me a kiss. And some dude, who from time to time argued that Shaun, Connor, Madeline Q, and Tayler would be insignificant to future generations, grinned at me as if he'd been tricked into discarding the perfect poker hand.

And I recognized many more the longer I studied that crowd. Mike looked over his shoulder, then back to me, smiling like the president of my fan club. And for a moment, I felt foolish for thinking at one time that he and the Alternative Net were another one of Stuart's mindless plans.

"I'm surprised to find you at the head of the flock, Mike," Stuart declared.

"I'm not like my father, I'm a humanitarian. I'm a writer."

"Save the clichés for your unread books."

Other guards were racing outside to join Stuart, including the punkish one I once kissed. They lifted their guns and aimed at the mass. Mike lifted his device as most of the others followed his lead. Shaun held the weapon steadily. Felicity huddled close to his side.

"We're streaming live," Mike announced.

"Why bother?" Stuart said. "You know I can shut down Social Media Central." He dug his hands deep into the pockets of his jacket. "Oh, I see. You're streaming on the Alta Net. Wow, all of Astra City must be glued to their screens."

"Hashtag, the Government. Trust me, you're trending on both your site and ours."

I took out my device and logged in. Sure enough, thousands were watching and about half of them were commenting. I viewed the next stream, then the next, where even more conversation was happening through SMC. I suddenly realized Stuart was glued to my display.

"So, Government..." I began speaking before I knew how to finish the sentence. "You think we are all insignificant? Well, let's talk. Let's find out how significant you are, Mr. Manning."

"These are stupid games, Tayler. A broadcast of something no one will understand."

"So, let's make them understand. Why did you put Connor, Shaun, Madeline Q, and me on your payroll?"

He glared as if a demon had jabbed him.

"Cat got your tongue?" I leaned toward him. "No one was noticing you, were they, Stuart? So you wanted us to be your spokespeople."

"You flatter yourself, Tayler. In fact, you *all* do. Connor, who lives for art. A thousand photos swallowed into cyberspace, forgotten in the archives of SMC. Shaun, whose exploits made virgins long for tenderness, as long as it could be found through a webcam. Oh, and Madeline Q. A pretentious name for a pretentious person. The queen of the narcissists, with followers flocking at her whim."

She spat at him, only to have three guards raise their guns.

"I've always loved your bravado, Madeline. It's a shame it couldn't be matched with substance."

"Stuart, it seems you avoided my accusations so you could dribble poison at the messengers formerly on your payroll."

"Sure, I can talk about Connor going off message. About the idiots of Astra City running home to chat to people they were never going to meet. About them having no idea what leaders are here for and what our roles are. About them finally communicating face to face over meals served at a restaurant. So what does it prove?"

"You hit on something a couple of sentences back." I glanced at the crowd, sensing their warmth in the brisk night air. I was standing on a make-believe platform without fear of making a fool of myself. I had a voice!

"Really? You think I said something worth repeating? But who are you to deem what's important or what's not? Tayler, my model geek, who had nothing to say on Social Media Central. And still hid behind anonymity on the Alta Net."

His words floated past my ears. They could not harm me. They were drifting out to an imaginary sea. I pictured Audrey, my fourth-grade teacher, listening as I gazed into my collective. I was her little boy worthy of being noticed.

I took time to gather my thoughts. We were joined by thirteen stragglers who had left their fake selves behind to see with their own eyes what was going on outside their compound.

"Let's dissect what you said, Stuart," I began. "You said the people of Astra City didn't know who you were. You said they didn't even know there was a leader in charge of their concerns."

He took a step back.

"Have you given them a reason to listen to you?"

Connor began to stand upright without the help of the guards. Madi folded her arms while sharing a look of pride.

"I'm the Government. The public should listen."

"But by your own admission, you said they didn't know you existed."

"How can the office of the Government survive when most of these fools don't know what my role is?"

More employees joined us outside, some recognizing others in the crowd.

"But you're not managing the city. You have no vision. You just want to be boss at any cost. Your ego is making you jump like a performing animal through any hoop you think will make people notice you. But the truth is, you're irrelevant. Not because we don't need leadership. Because you don't lead. And any amount of wasting money, on this idiotic scheme or that, just won't make you relevant. Inspire these people by example and they'll notice."

Our silent audience suddenly cheered at deafening levels.

"Hear that, Stuart? That's the sound of your own personal failure."

"You are talking out of your ass, little boy Tayler!"

"Oh, come on, Mr. Government, what's one policy you've come up with to make these people's lives better?"

"Sounds like you've discovered the Alta Net," said Connor. I nodded briefly.

"Stop this carnival ride. I want to get off." The leader's voice quivered as he spoke.

"You were never on that ride," I said. "You just wanted the title, but not the job that went with it. You told us so yourself."

Stuart raised his hand, but I didn't budge. He lowered it.

"Did you run education? Did you increase wealth for your citizens? Did you feed us? Clothe us? Or did you just stand by and criticize us, because you really had nothing else to do?"

"No, Tayler, he did none of what the great leaders of the past had done," said Connor. "So no one noticed him no matter how many times we mentioned him, because he made himself irrelevant."

"If someone your age still feels they're a nobody, Stuart, it's fair to say all you really wanted was what some of us already had. Celebrity!"

"Take them captive, Number Thirteen," he commanded. "And the rest of you, aim your guns at this idiotic crowd and bring them inside."

Shaun stepped forward, holding his firearm higher toward the fledgling leader. But his gesture was unnecessary, for Number Thirteen was aiming squarely at the center of Stuart's face.

"What are you doing, you useless beast?" he cried.

"Too many deaths have resulted through your madness," the guard said.

"You just turned against me because of your kissy-kissy session with Tayler."

"No, I'm sick of being called Number Thirteen. I do have a name. We all do."

One of the other guards raised his gun to Stuart's back. Gasps came as a chorus from the mob. Next, the two that had assisted Connor followed Number Thirteen's lead. One by one, the guards found their conscience, stepping up to the madman and surrounding him.

"You despicable..."

We waited politely for him to finish his sentence, but he uttered nothing more.

"There's one more thing we need to do, Tayler," said Connor.

"I think I'm on your wavelength. Be my guest."

I gestured for him to step in front of me.

He stood tall, proudly addressing the eager audience. "You've all read the archival documents on the Alta Net. You must have realized that computers have sped up their own evolution, making us less relevant. They've isolated us, bringing us closer to our demise."

Many shared puzzled looks.

"The devices in your hands think for us. They watch us. They give us no anonymity." Now even more glanced at each other as if Connor was talking a foreign language.

"Listen, guys," I said. "Take a good look at those windows to your worlds. Go on. I dare you. Try your hardest." About half complied, but only after discreet nods from those that kept streaming. "They haven't made you freer. They've made your generation and your parents' generation more conservative. None of you are as deep as you should be. None of you understand life like your ancestors did, including me."

Madi stepped forward. "Everyone hug the person next to you," she said. Again there were mystified looks. She wrapped her arms around me.

"Oh, you make me sick," Stuart squealed.

As Madi held me tighter, more and more of the crowd complied. A greasy-haired teen was squeezed by a busty woman in glasses. A pudgy couple weren't quite sure how to cuddle as their arms made strange movements, one almost poking the other in the eye. Hesitantly, they relaxed into their embrace. And an older couple closed their eyes as they swayed in each other's arms. As the love poured steadily through the crowd, Mike gave me the look of someone who had just been told he'd been adopted.

"Now turn around and introduce yourself to someone you don't know," I shouted. "Hug them. Let's get back to real emotion. Let's sense real touch."

Shaun cheered at this point.

"Let's have real discussions about our inherent sense of emptiness."

As I gestured for Mike to join me, Madi pulled away. And while he made his way to my side, a smashing sound came from the crowd. The others turned to reveal a guy younger than me with his device in pieces at his feet. Instantly, another screen hit the ground. Then another, creating a chaotic symphony that sounded oh so sweet. I studied mine with its stylish metallic case before it too died a public death.

"You still need someone to be in charge of you rebels," said Stuart. He sneered at the crowd.

Once more, they called my name. They followed this with three claps and then yelled my name again. Then they repeated this pattern over and over again. "Tayler!" *Clap. Clap. Clap.* "Tayler!" *Clap. Clap. Clap.*

Connor grinned, but I shook my head. I gazed into the audience and then gestured toward Connor. If anyone could play the Government, this was their man. He was well-read, and he was a silent student of human nature as seen through his art. A man with ideas and a man with concern.

Soon the cries of "Tayler!" switched to supporting calls for Connor. I'd never seen him so self-assured.

Behind me, more staff had left their fake identities behind. The façade was over. Some of the mob booed these tricksters, but they gradually made their way into the crowd to show their solidarity.

I asked Number Thirteen to take Stuart inside at gunpoint. I led the way as several renegade guards ushered him behind me. Madi and Mike followed.

We stepped into the massive room, now nearly empty with most of its workers outside. We listened, hearing those still in their rooms confessing their deceit to the people at home. Someone even criticized Stuart for his power-hungry nature. There must have been intrigue in hearing an insider's view.

"In here," I said to the fallen leader. I picked one of the stylish rooms. A plush white modular sofa made its presence felt as the centerpiece. "No, don't sit on the couch. Crouch in front of the computer."

"This is childish," he barked.

The guards shoved their guns against his body. With his last shred of elegance, he lowered himself onto his knees. Madi and Mike watched me from the entrance like proud parents.

"See this thing in front of you, Stuart? It's called a computer. You could have sat in front of one of these and talked to people one on one. It's really quite simple. You could have met them personally and seen what they needed from you, what they needed from their government."

I found a group talk session and logged in. A live stream of three faces who had been captivated by the live events, now appeared on the screen.

I made sure Stuart was right in front of the webcam so they could see him clearly, along with the guns that were keeping him in place. He looked as confused as the group we'd gatecrashed.

I faced the camera, smiling over his shoulder. "Meet one of the minor influences. The one with the least followers."

I left him and walked outside with my arms around my two lovers. The crowd was chatting eagerly with their once-fake counterparts. Some workers defended their actions, while others were holding court with their own captive audience.

But my thoughts were drifting. On either side of me stood a person who'd shown me love, then made me suspicious of its nature.

Mike had tears rolling down his cheeks. As he wiped them away, his crying turned to laughter. I ran my fingers through his shaggy hair and kissed his coward-lion grin. He tasted bristly, tender, and safe.

Madi, on the other hand, stood proud. Madeline Q had been left far behind, and the woman that hid behind her mask had come out from her shadow. I lifted my finger and rested it on the bottom of her chin and then eased her to my lips. I savored her scent.

Through this, I delighted in the fact I had a choice to make. A choice between the one who'd lived the dream until her silent years connected with my solitude, or the one that understood my isolation from day one, drawing me out of my shell one step at a time.

And I found joy in the fact I lived an existence that gave me this authentic decision to make. One I didn't have to post for advice, soliciting comments from those who knew no better. I felt justified in knowing what it meant to be human and it had nothing to do with swiping a screen, tapping a keyboard, or clicking a mouse.

# About the Author

Kevin is the author of a number of books including the Actors and Angels series and the Nate and Cameron Collection.

The Actors and Angels series are three comedies about theatre in the Afterlife, where two friends explore their love for each other through several lifetimes with the help of a gay angel. The third in the series scored a Rainbow Award for Best Gay Alternative Universe/Reality novel.

The Nate and Cameron collection are two novellas that delve into a relationship between a dreamer and a realist, where the latter is coming to terms with loving second best. The two stories, *Nate and the New Yorker* and *Nate's Last Tango*, are also available in one paperback edition.

Kevin lives with his long-term partner, Warren, in their humble apartment (affectionately named Sabrina), in Australia's own "Emerald City," Sydney.

Facebook:
www.facebook.com/DramaQueensWithLoveScenes

Twitter: @kevinklehr

Website: www.kevinklehr.com

Instagram: www.instagram.com/klehrkevin

# Other books by this author

Actors and Angels Series
*Drama Queens with Love Scenes*
*Drama Queens and Adult Themes*
*Drama Queens and Devilish Schemes*

Nate and Cameron Series
*Nate and the New Yorker*
*Nate's Last Tango*
*The Nate and Cameron Collection* (Paperback only)

*From Top to Bottom*

# Also Available from NineStar Press

# Connect with NineStar Press

www.ninestarpress.com

www.facebook.com/ninestarpress

www.facebook.com/groups/NineStarNiche

www.twitter.com/ninestarpress

www.tumblr.com/blog/ninestarpress